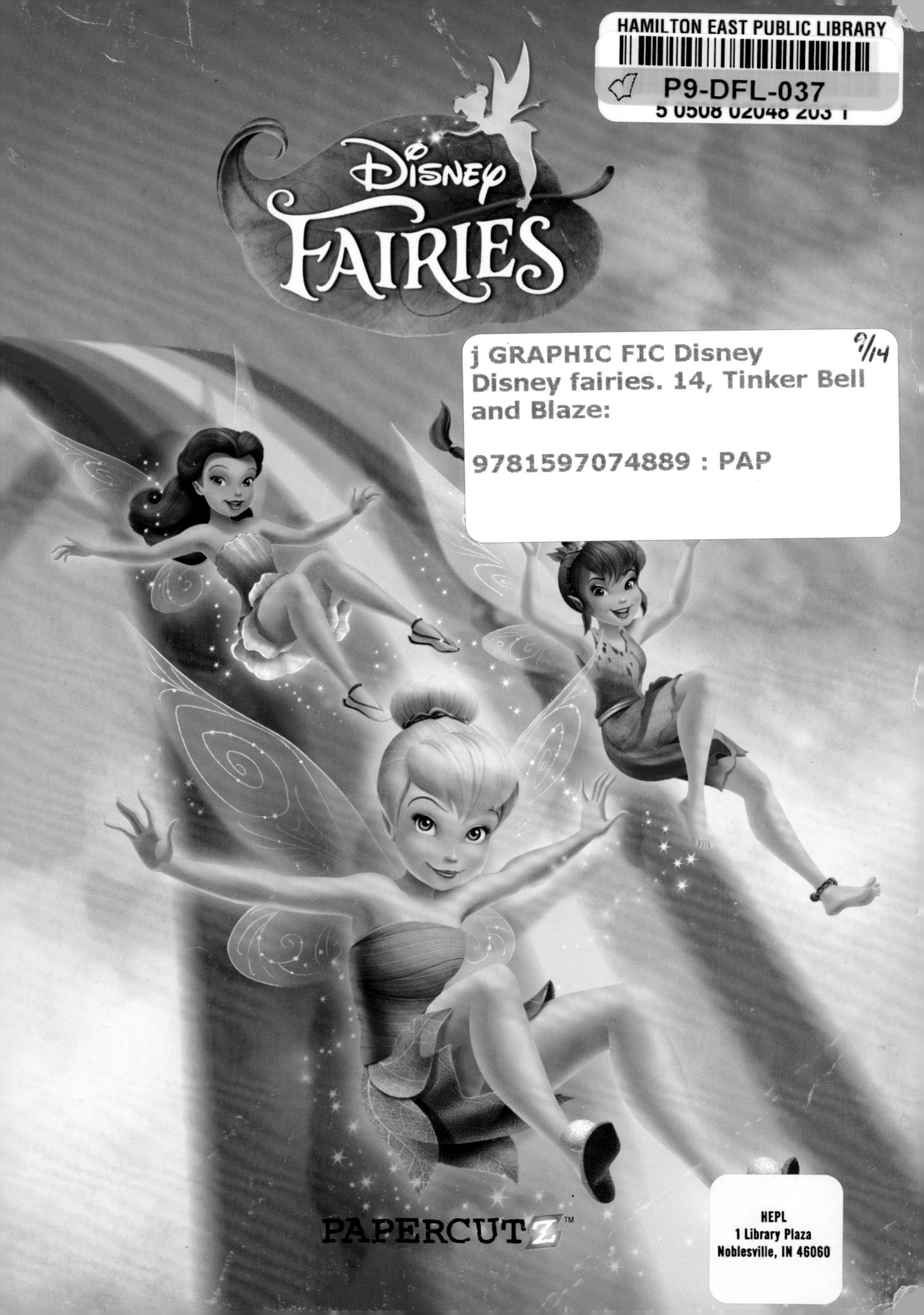
Disney
FAIRIES
PAPERCUTZ™

Graphic Novels Available from
PAPERCUTZ

Graphic Novel #1
"Prilla's Talent"

Graphic Novel #2
"Tinker Bell and the
Wings of Rani"

Graphic Novel #3
"Tinker Bell and the Day
of the Dragon"

Graphic Novel #4
"Tinker Bell
to the Rescue"

Graphic Novel #5
"Tinker Bell and
the Pirate Adventure"

Graphic Novel #6
"A Present
for Tinker Bell"

Graphic Novel #7
"Tinker Bell the
Perfect Fairy"

Graphic Novel #8
"Tinker Bell and her
Stories for a Rainy Day"

Graphic Novel #9
"Tinker Bell and
her Magical Arrival"

Graphic Novel #10
"Tinker Bell and
the Lucky Rainbow"

Graphic Novel #11
"Tinker Bell and the
Most Precious Gift"

Graphic Novel #12
"Tinker Bell and the
Lost Treasure"

Graphic Novel #13
"Tinker Bell and the
Pixie Hollow Games"

Graphic Novel #14
"Tinker Bell and Blaze"

**Tinker Bell and the
Great Fairy Rescue**

COMING SOON

Graphic Novel #15
"Tinker Bell and the
Secret of the Wings"

DISNEY FAIRIES graphic novels are available in paperback for $7.99 each;
in hardcover for $12.99 each except #5, $6.99PB, $10.99HC. #6-15 are $7.99PB $11.99HC.
Tinker Bell and the Great Fairy Rescue is $9.99 in hardcover only.
Available at booksellers everywhere.

See more at papercutz.com

Or you can order from us: Please add $4.00 for postage and handling for first book, and add $1.00 for each
additional book. Please make check payable to NBM Publishing. Send to: Papercutz, 160 Broadway, Suite
700, East Wing, New York, NY 10038 or call 800 886 1223 (9-6 EST M-F) MC-Visa-Amex accepted.

Disney FAIRIES

#14 "Tinker Bell and Blaze"

Contents

PAPERCUTZ™

NEW YORK

"Once Upon a Time"
Script: Emanuela Portipiano
Revised Dialogue: Cortney Faye Powell
Pencils: Manuela Razzi
Inks: Roberta Zanotta
Color: Studio Kawaii
Letters: Janice Chiang
Page 5 Art:
Concept: Tea Orsi
Layout: Monica Catalano
Pencils: Marino Gentile
Color: Andrea Cagol

"Remember Me"
Script: Tea Orsi
Revised Dialogue: Cortney Faye Powell
Pencils: Caterina Giorgilli
Inks: Roberta Zanotta
Color: Studio Kawaii
Letters: Janice Chiang
Page 10 Art:
Concept: Tea Orsi
Pencils and Inks: Sara Storino
Color: Andrea Cagol

"Misunderstood Style"
Script: Tea Orsi
Revised Dialogue: Cortney Faye Powell
Pencils: Manuela Razzi
Inks: Roberta Zanotta
Color: Studio Kawaii
Letters: Janice Chiang

"The Shiny Thing"
Script: Carlo Panaro
Revised Dialogue: Cortney Faye Powell
Pencils: Manuela Razzi
Inks: Roberta Zanotta
Color: Studio Kawaii
Letters: Janice Chiang

"A Fast-flying Fairy Shows her True Colors"
Script: Carlo Panaro
Revised Dialogue: Cortney Faye Powell
Pencils and Inks: Monica Catalano
Color: Studio Kawaii
Letters: Janice Chiang
Page 23 Art:
Layout, Pencils and Inks: Sara Storino
Color: Andrea Cagol

"The Missing Butterfly"
Script: Tea Orsi
Revised Dialogue: Cortney Faye Powell
Pencils and Inks: Monica Catalano
Color: Studio Kawaii
Letters: Janice Chiang

"The Bad Mannered Blossom"
Script: Tea Orsi
Revised Dialogue: Cortney Faye Powell
Pencils: Manuela Razzi
Inks: Marina Baggio
Color: Studio Kawaii
Letters: Janice Chiang
Page 32 Art:
Concept: Caterina Giorgetti
Pencils and Inks: Sara Storino
Color: Andrea Cagol

"False Alarm!"
Script: Emanuela Portipiano
Revised Dialogue: Cortney Faye Powell
Pencils: Sara Storino
Inks: Roberta Zanotta
Color: Studio Kawaii
Letters: Janice Chiang
Page 37 Art:
Pencils & Inks: Marino Gentile &
Sara Storino
Color: Mara Damiani &
Stefano Attardi

"A Strange, Strange Star"
Script: Tea Orsi
Revised Dialogue: Cortney Faye Powell
Pencils: Manuela Razzi
Inks: Roberta Zanotta
Color: Studio Kawaii
Letters: Janice Chiang
Page 42 Art:
Concept: Tea Orsi
Pencils and Inks: Sara Storino
Color: Andrea Cagol

"The Long, Long Night"
Script: Emanuela Portipiano
Revised Dialogue: Cortney Faye Powell
Pencils: Manuela Razzi
Inks: Roberta Zanotta
Color: Studio Kawaii
Letters: Janice Chiang
Page 47 Art:
Concept: Tea Orsi
Pencils and Inks: Sara Storino
Color: Andrea Cagol

"A Starless Night"
Script: Carlo Panaro
Revised Dialogue: Cortney Faye Powell
Pencils: Sara Storino
Inks: Roberta Zanotta
Color: Studio Kawaii
Letters: Janice Chiang
Page 52 Art:
Concept: Tea Orsi
Pencils and Inks: Sara Storino
Color: Andrea Cagol

"An Unexpected Adventure"
Script: Carlo Panaro
Revised Dialogue: Cortney Faye Powell
Pencils: Mario Gentile
Inks: Roberta Zanotta
Color: Studio Kawaii
Letters: Janice Chiang
Page 57 Art:
Concept: Tea Orsi
Pencils and Inks: Sara Storino
Color: Andrea Cagol

Production – Dawn K. Guzzo
Special Thanks – Sara Srisoonthorn
Production Coordinator – Beth Scorzato
Associate Editor – Michael Petranek
Jim Salicrup
Editor-in-Chief

ISBN: 978-1-59707-488-9 paperback edition
ISBN: 978-1-59707-489-6 hardcover edition

Printed in China
April 2014 by Asia One Printing LTD
13/F Asia One Tower
8 Fung Yip St., Chaiwan
Hong Kong

Papercutz books may be purchased for business or promotional use. For information on bulk purchases please contact Macmillan Corporate and Premium Sales Department at (800) 221-7945 x5442.

Distributed by Macmillan
First Papercutz Printing

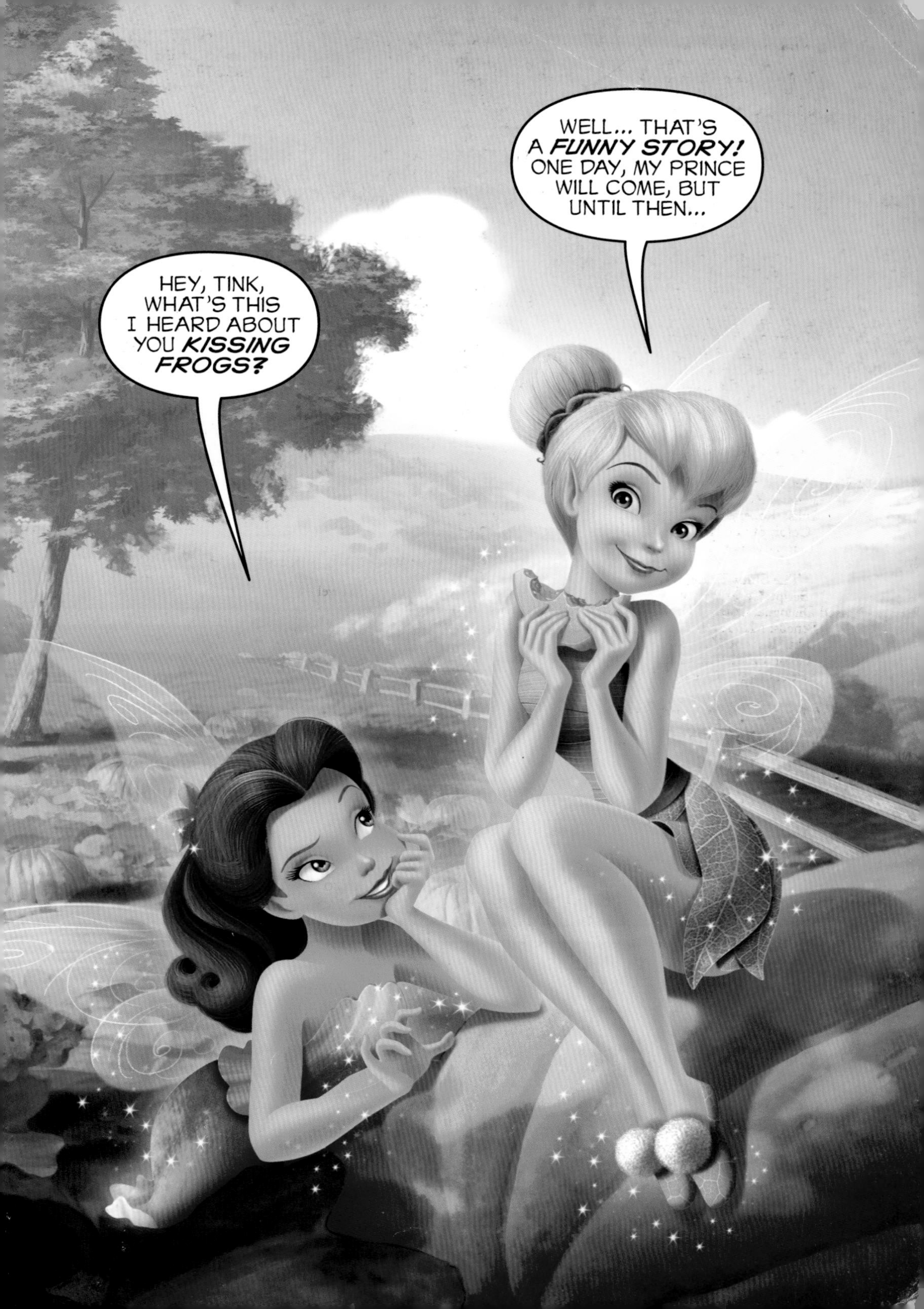
HEY, TINK, WHAT'S THIS I HEARD ABOUT YOU *KISSING FROGS?*
WELL... THAT'S A *FUNNY STORY!* ONE DAY, MY PRINCE WILL COME, BUT UNTIL THEN...

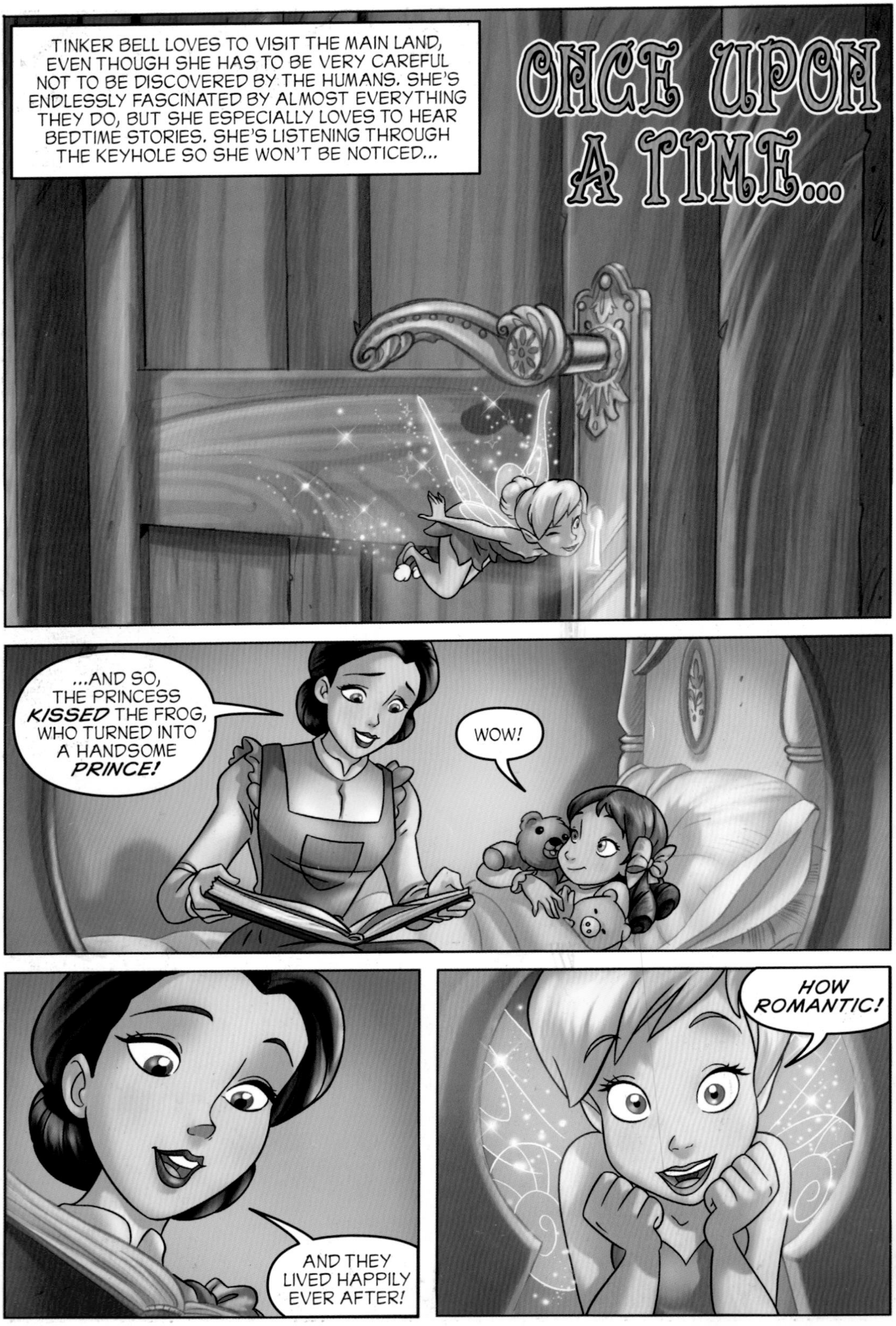
TINKER BELL LOVES TO VISIT THE MAIN LAND, EVEN THOUGH SHE HAS TO BE VERY CAREFUL NOT TO BE DISCOVERED BY THE HUMANS. SHE'S ENDLESSLY FASCINATED BY ALMOST EVERYTHING THEY DO, BUT SHE ESPECIALLY LOVES TO HEAR BEDTIME STORIES. SHE'S LISTENING THROUGH THE KEYHOLE SO SHE WON'T BE NOTICED...
ONCE UPON A TIME...
...AND SO, THE PRINCESS KISSED THE FROG, WHO TURNED INTO A HANDSOME PRINCE!
WOW!
AND THEY LIVED HAPPILY EVER AFTER!
HOW ROMANTIC!

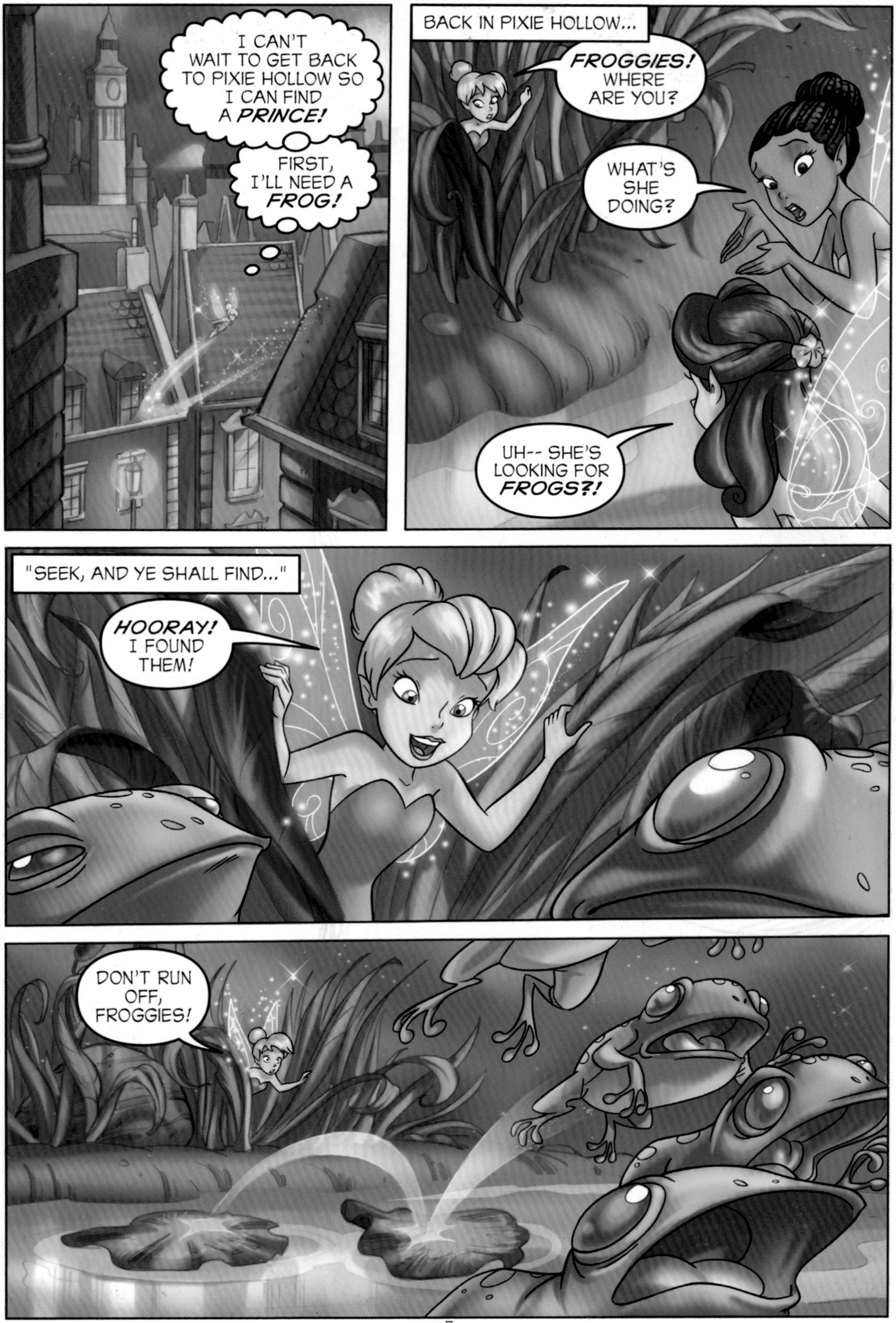
I CAN'T WAIT TO GET BACK TO PIXIE HOLLOW SO I CAN FIND A *PRINCE!*
FIRST, I'LL NEED A *FROG!*
BACK IN PIXIE HOLLOW...
FROGGIES! WHERE ARE YOU?
WHAT'S SHE DOING?
UH-- SHE'S LOOKING FOR *FROGS?!*
"SEEK, AND YE SHALL FIND..."
HOORAY! I FOUND THEM!
DON'T RUN OFF, FROGGIES!

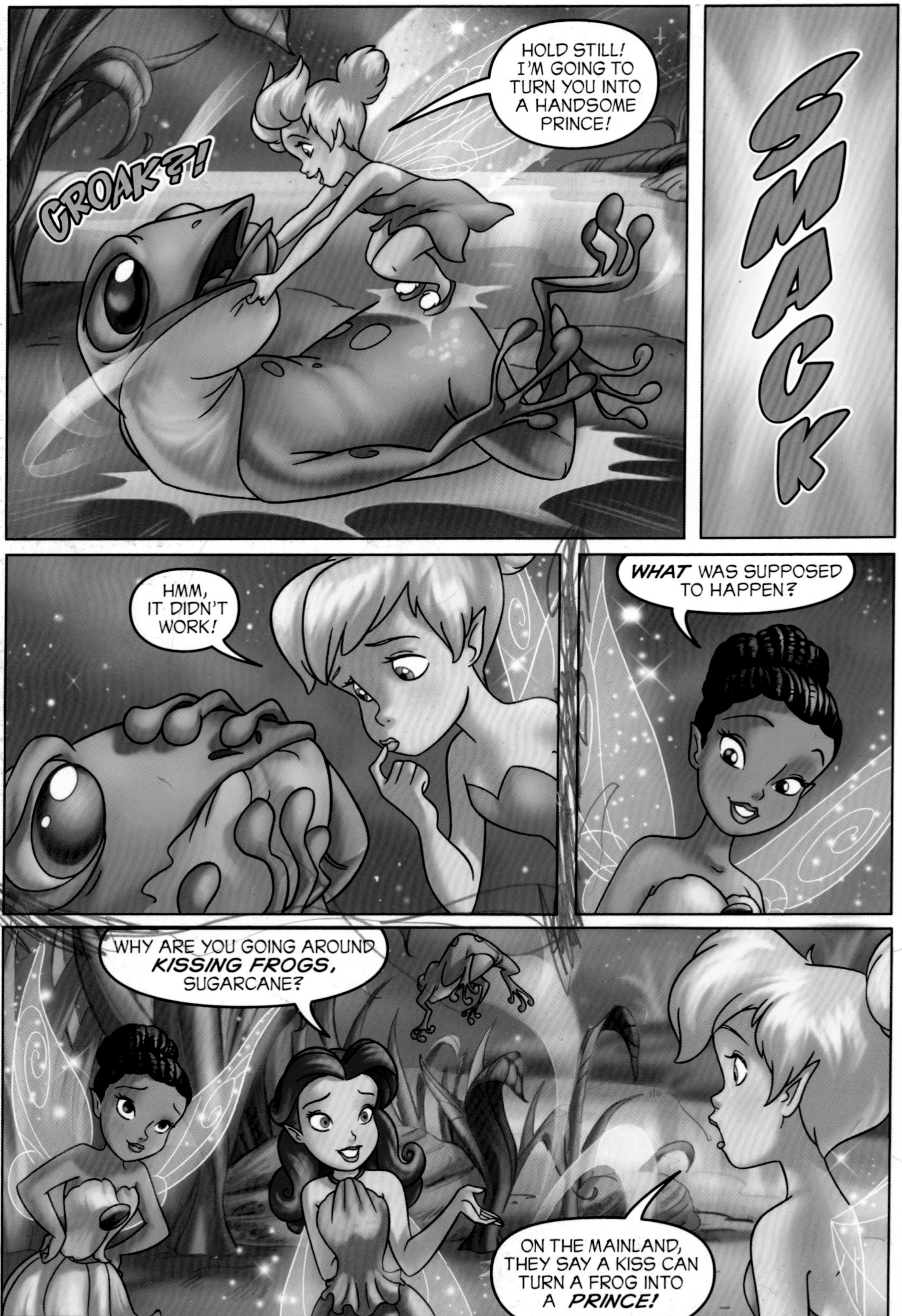
HOLD STILL! I'M GOING TO TURN YOU INTO A HANDSOME PRINCE!
CROAK?!
SMACK
HMM, IT DIDN'T WORK!
WHAT WAS SUPPOSED TO HAPPEN?
WHY ARE YOU GOING AROUND KISSING FROGS, SUGARCANE?
ON THE MAINLAND, THEY SAY A KISS CAN TURN A FROG INTO A PRINCE!

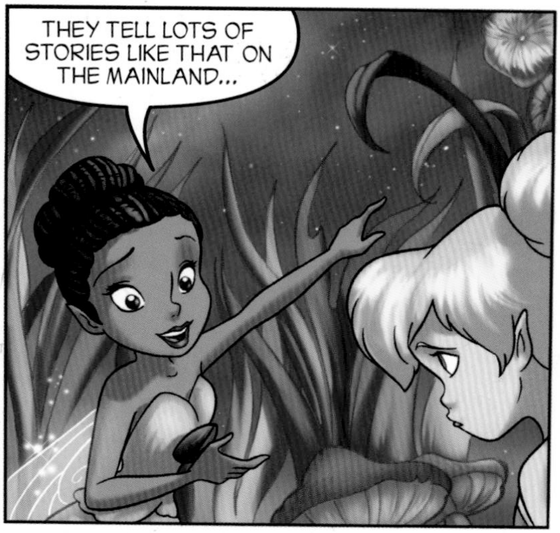
THEY TELL LOTS OF STORIES LIKE THAT ON THE MAINLAND...
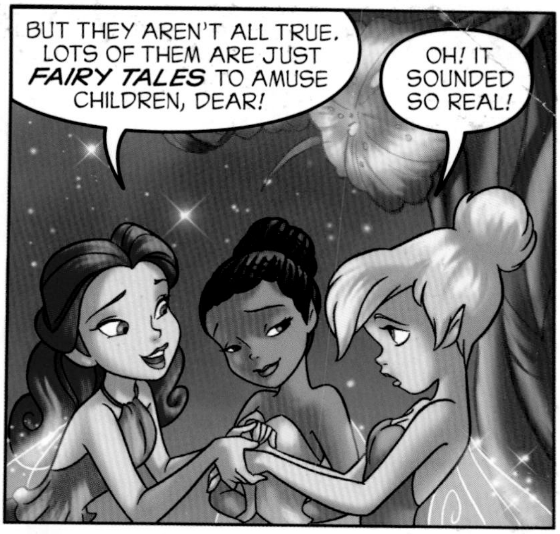
BUT THEY AREN'T ALL TRUE. LOTS OF THEM ARE JUST *FAIRY TALES* TO AMUSE CHILDREN, DEAR!
OH! IT SOUNDED SO REAL!
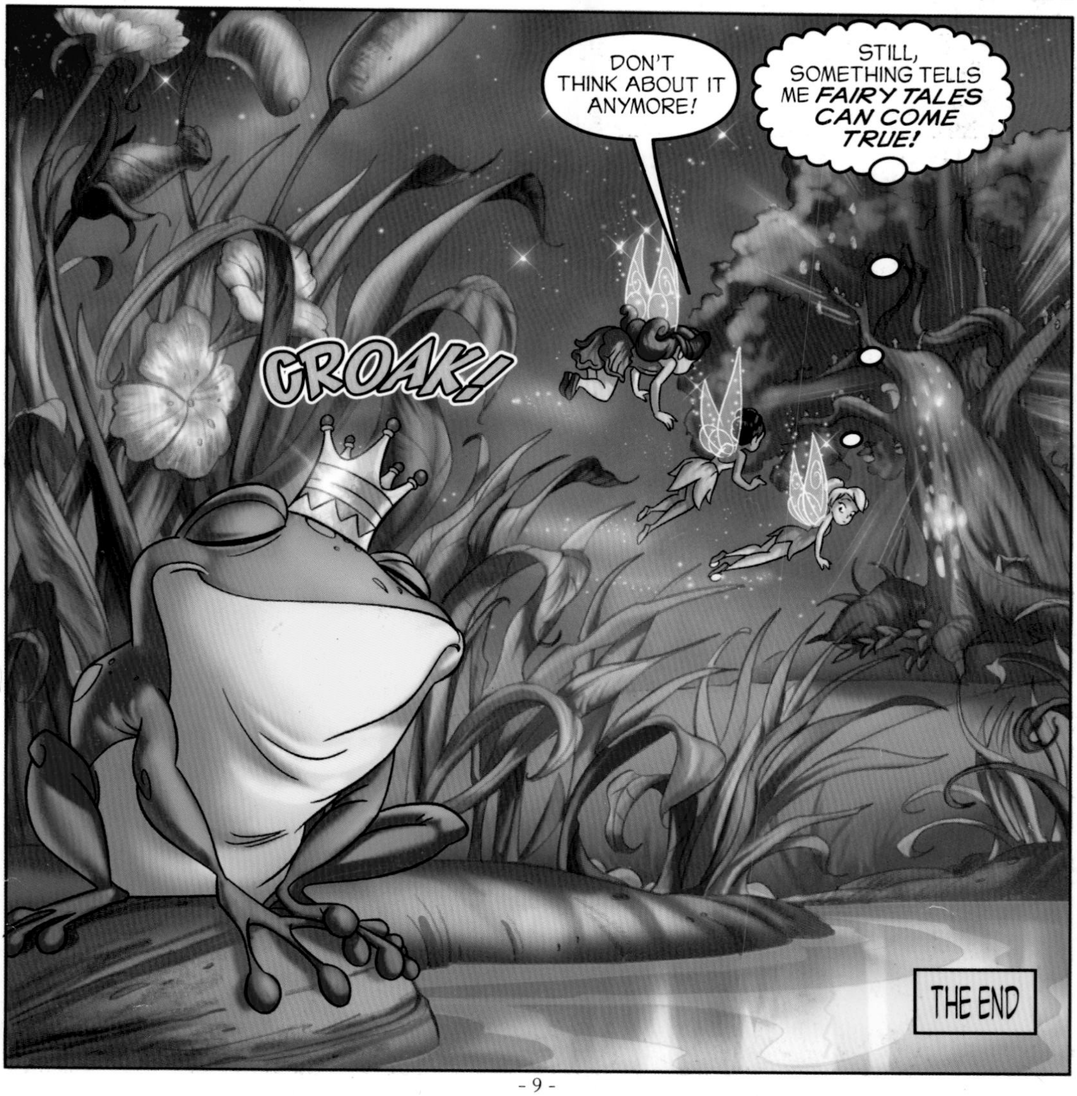
DON'T THINK ABOUT IT ANYMORE!
STILL, SOMETHING TELLS ME *FAIRY TALES CAN COME TRUE!*
CROAK!
THE END

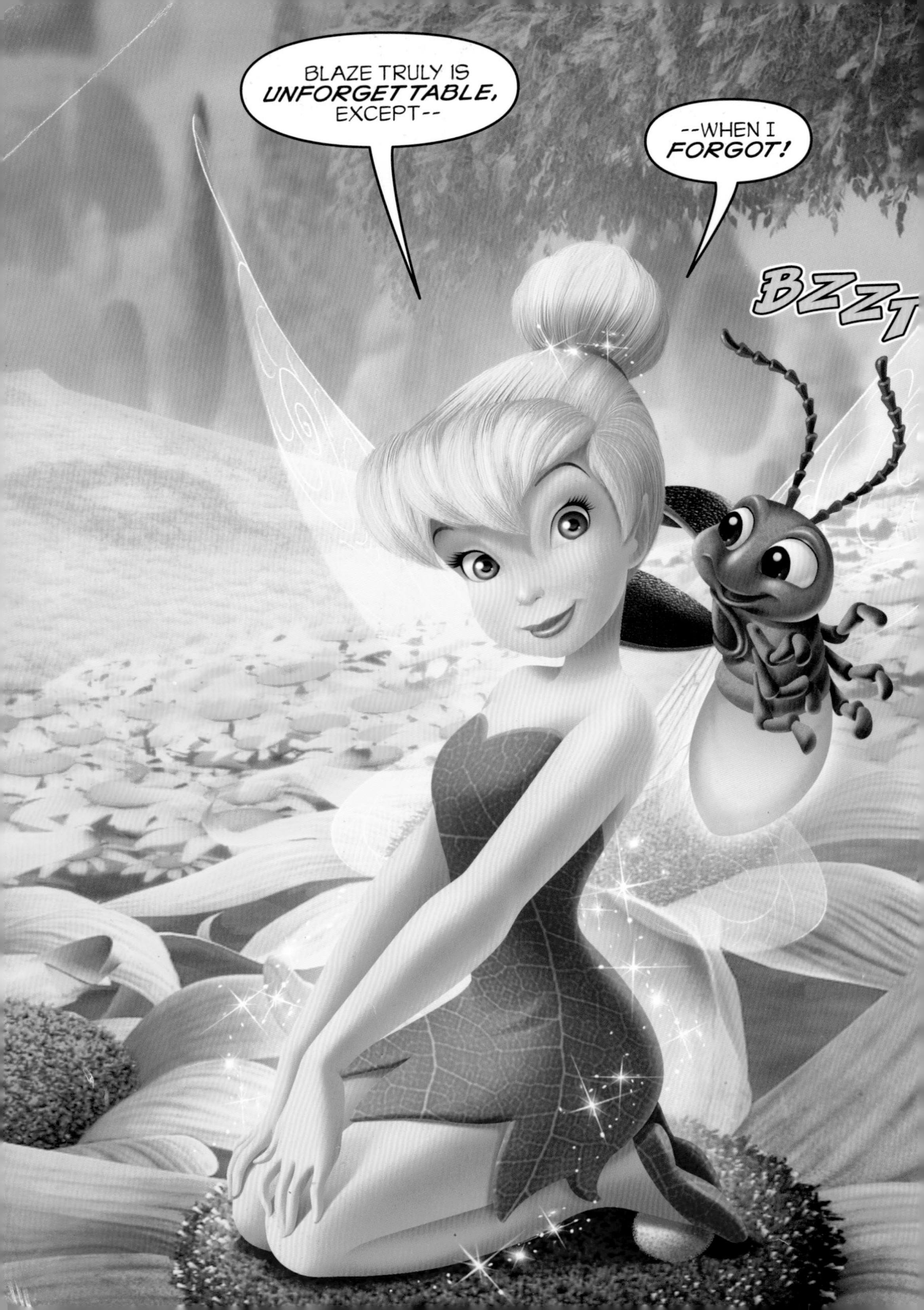

BLAZE TRULY IS *UNFORGETTABLE,* EXCEPT--
--WHEN I *FORGOT!*
BZZT

REMEMBER ME!

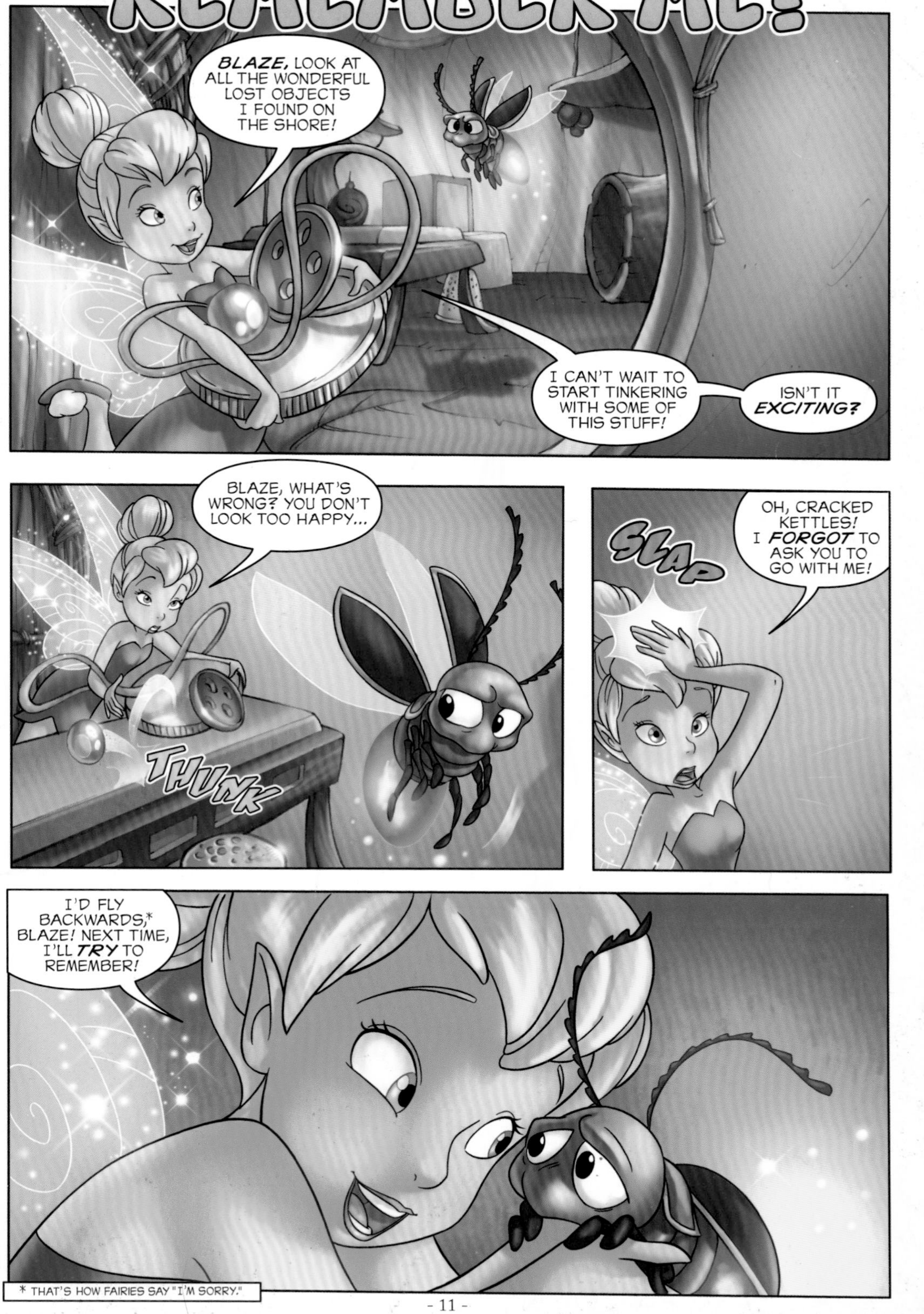
BLAZE, LOOK AT ALL THE WONDERFUL LOST OBJECTS I FOUND ON THE SHORE!
I CAN'T WAIT TO START TINKERING WITH SOME OF THIS STUFF!
ISN'T IT EXCITING?
BLAZE, WHAT'S WRONG? YOU DON'T LOOK TOO HAPPY...
THUNK
SLAP
OH, CRACKED KETTLES! I FORGOT TO ASK YOU TO GO WITH ME!
I'D FLY BACKWARDS,* BLAZE! NEXT TIME, I'LL TRY TO REMEMBER!

* THAT'S HOW FAIRIES SAY "I'M SORRY."

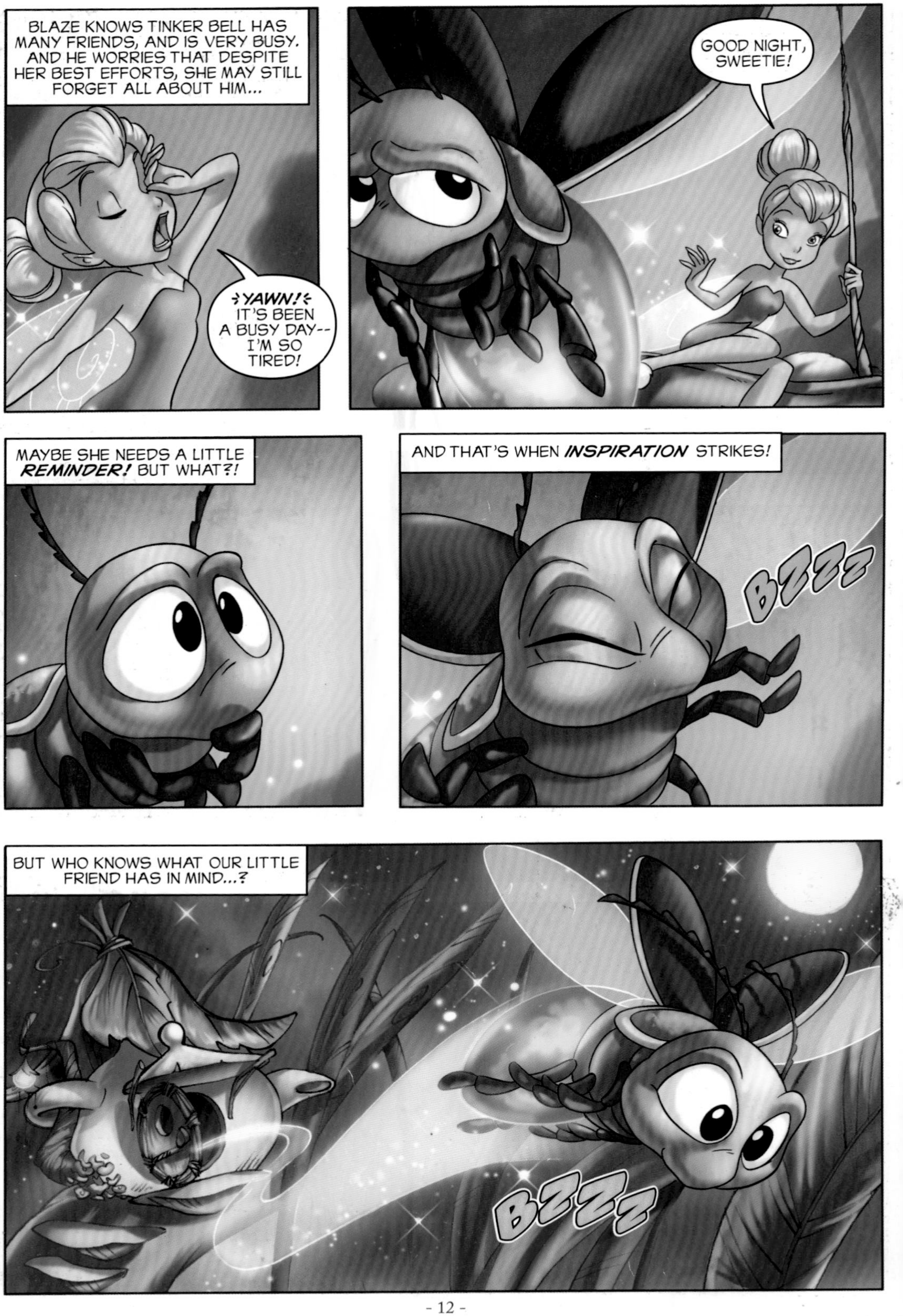
BLAZE KNOWS TINKER BELL HAS MANY FRIENDS, AND IS VERY BUSY. AND HE WORRIES THAT DESPITE HER BEST EFFORTS, SHE MAY STILL FORGET ALL ABOUT HIM...
YAWN! IT'S BEEN A BUSY DAY-- I'M SO TIRED!
GOOD NIGHT, SWEETIE!
MAYBE SHE NEEDS A LITTLE REMINDER! BUT WHAT?!
AND THAT'S WHEN INSPIRATION STRIKES!
BZZZ
BUT WHO KNOWS WHAT OUR LITTLE FRIEND HAS IN MIND...?
BZZZ

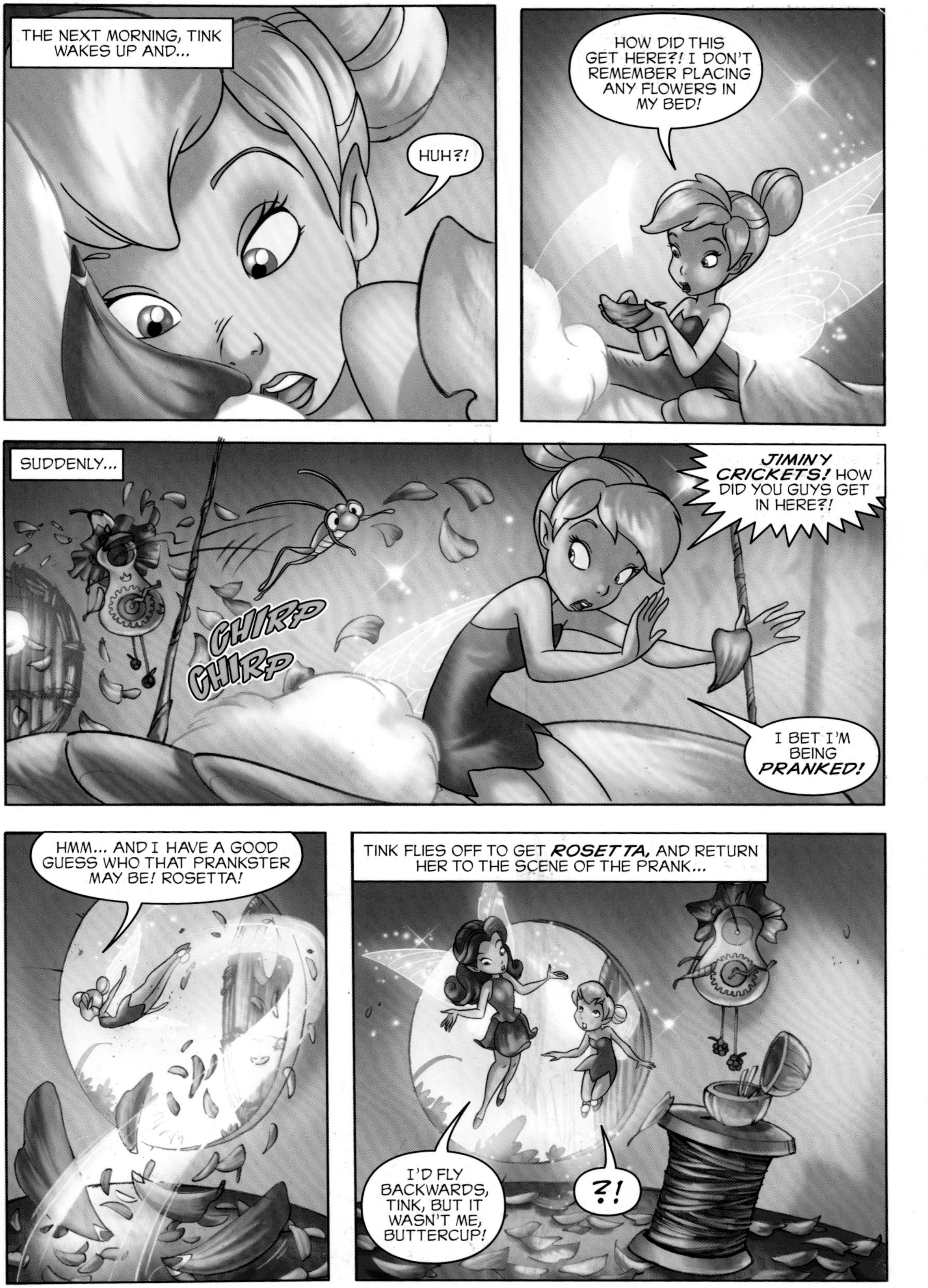
THE NEXT MORNING, TINK WAKES UP AND...
HUH?!
HOW DID THIS GET HERE?! I DON'T REMEMBER PLACING ANY FLOWERS IN MY BED!
SUDDENLY...
JIMINY CRICKETS! HOW DID YOU GUYS GET IN HERE?!
CHIRP CHIRP
I BET I'M BEING PRANKED!
HMM... AND I HAVE A GOOD GUESS WHO THAT PRANKSTER MAY BE! ROSETTA!
TINK FLIES OFF TO GET ROSETTA, AND RETURN HER TO THE SCENE OF THE PRANK...
I'D FLY BACKWARDS, TINK, BUT IT WASN'T ME, BUTTERCUP!
?!

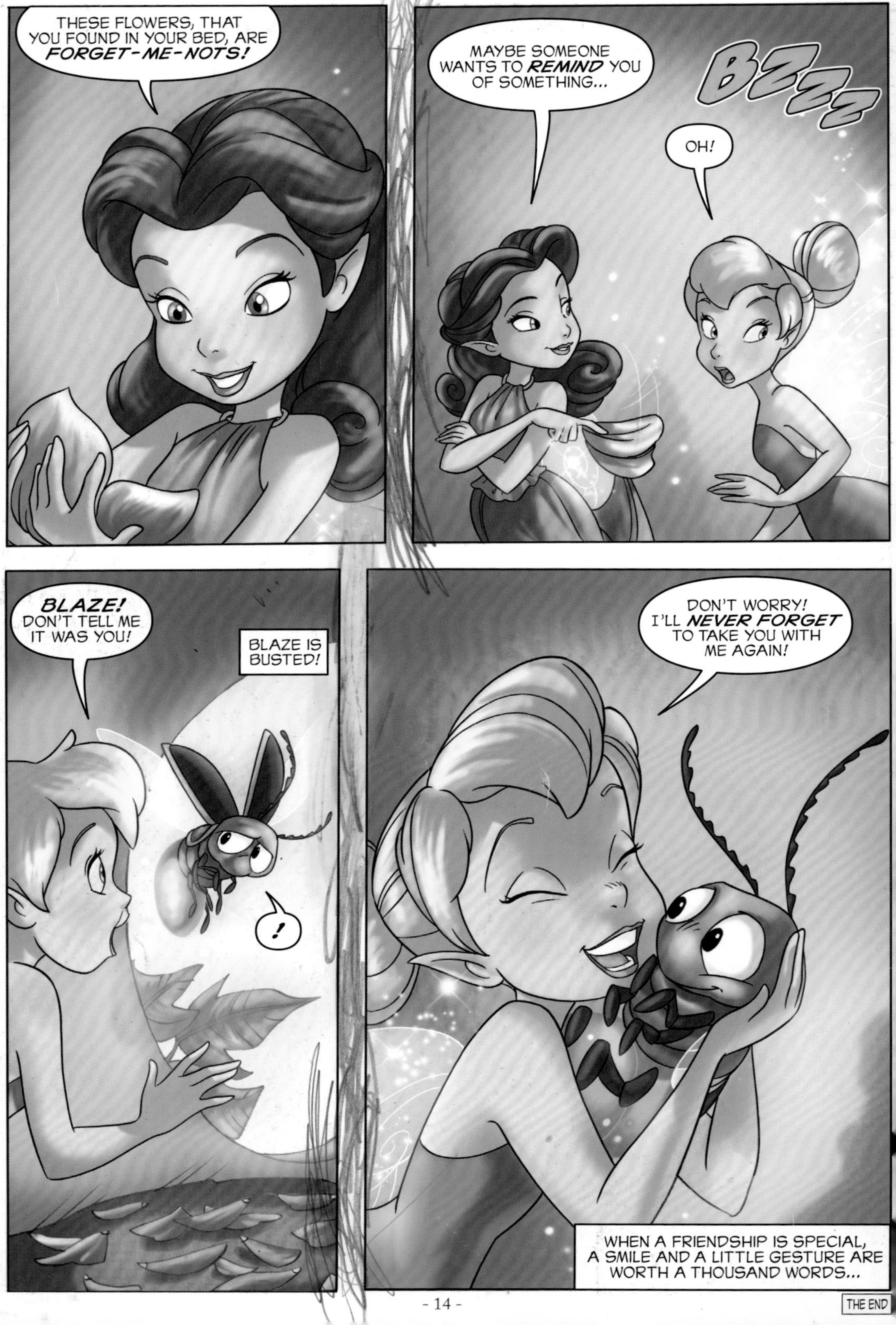
THESE FLOWERS, THAT YOU FOUND IN YOUR BED, ARE *FORGET-ME-NOTS!*
MAYBE SOMEONE WANTS TO *REMIND* YOU OF SOMETHING...
BZZZ
OH!
BLAZE! DON'T TELL ME IT WAS YOU!
BLAZE IS BUSTED!
!
DON'T WORRY! I'LL *NEVER FORGET* TO TAKE YOU WITH ME AGAIN!
WHEN A FRIENDSHIP IS SPECIAL, A SMILE AND A LITTLE GESTURE ARE WORTH A THOUSAND WORDS...
THE END

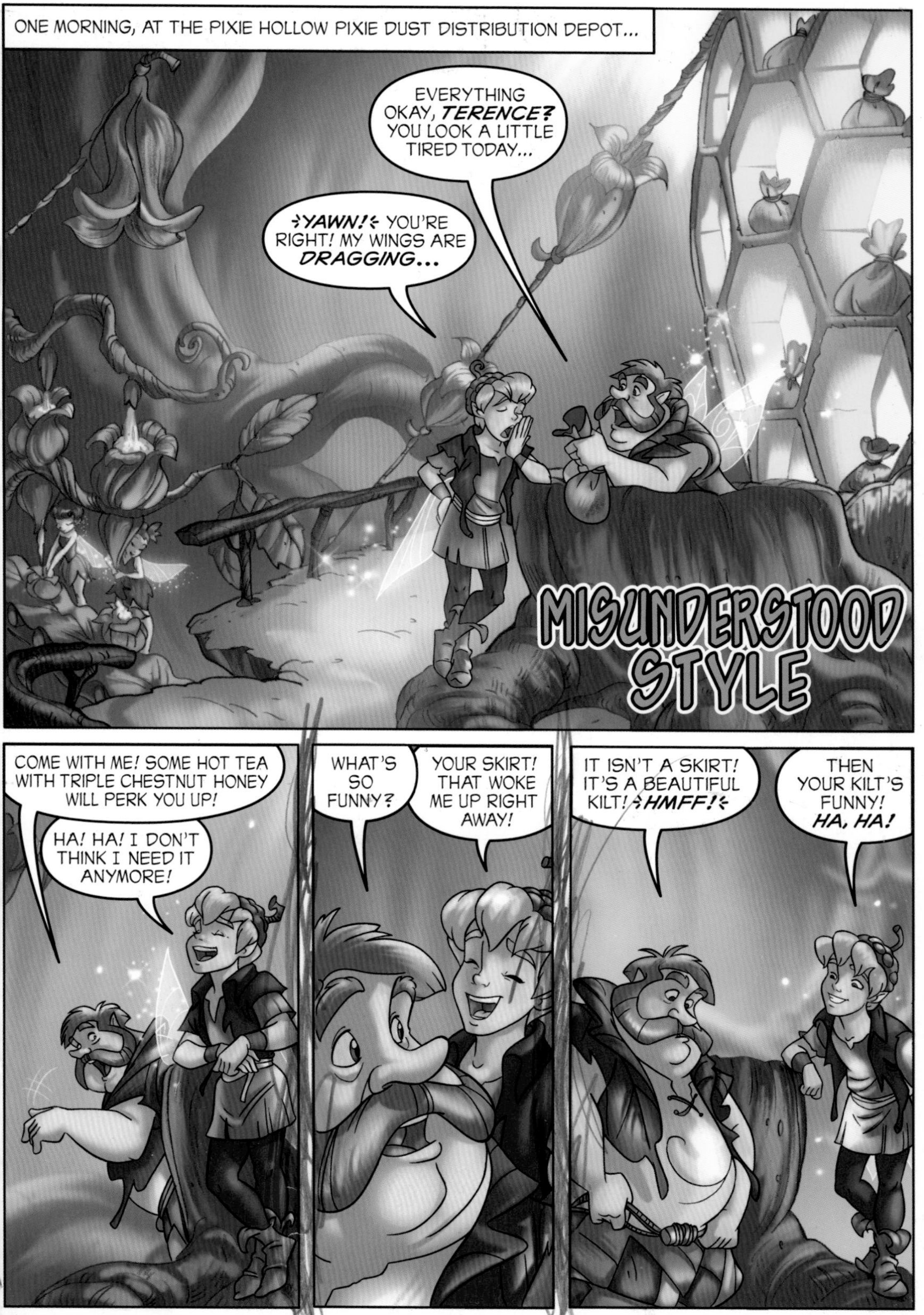
ONE MORNING, AT THE PIXIE HOLLOW PIXIE DUST DISTRIBUTION DEPOT...
EVERYTHING OKAY, TERENCE? YOU LOOK A LITTLE TIRED TODAY...
YAWN! YOU'RE RIGHT! MY WINGS ARE DRAGGING...
MISUNDERSTOOD STYLE
COME WITH ME! SOME HOT TEA WITH TRIPLE CHESTNUT HONEY WILL PERK YOU UP!
HA! HA! I DON'T THINK I NEED IT ANYMORE!
WHAT'S SO FUNNY?
YOUR SKIRT! THAT WOKE ME UP RIGHT AWAY!
IT ISN'T A SKIRT! IT'S A BEAUTIFUL KILT! HMFF!
THEN YOUR KILT'S FUNNY! HA, HA!

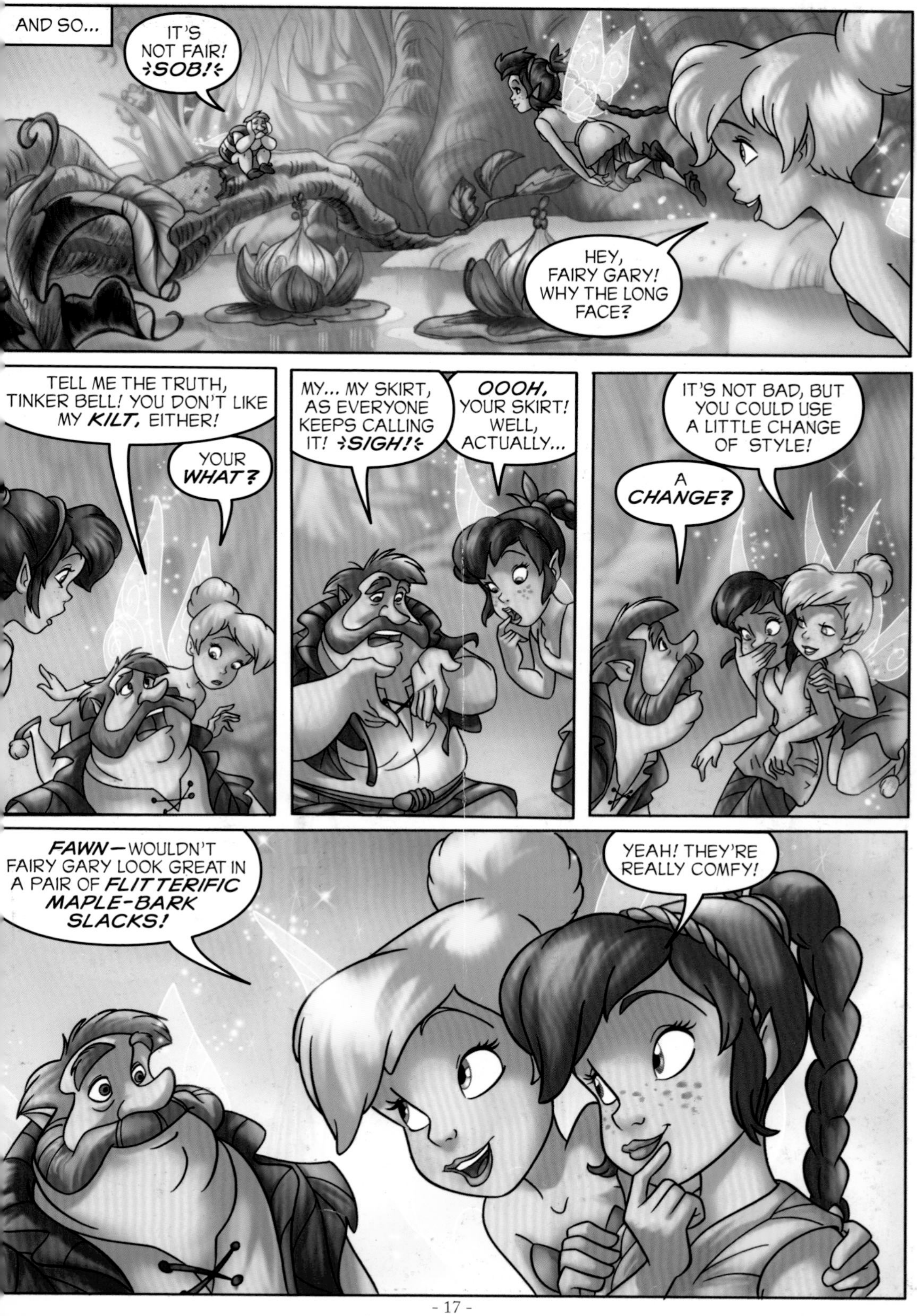
AND SO...
IT'S NOT FAIR! ⇶SOB!⇶
HEY, FAIRY GARY! WHY THE LONG FACE?
TELL ME THE TRUTH, TINKER BELL! YOU DON'T LIKE MY *KILT,* EITHER!
YOUR *WHAT?*
MY... MY SKIRT, AS EVERYONE KEEPS CALLING IT! *SIGH!*
OOOH, YOUR SKIRT! WELL, ACTUALLY...
IT'S NOT BAD, BUT YOU COULD USE A LITTLE CHANGE OF STYLE!
A *CHANGE?*
FAWN—WOULDN'T FAIRY GARY LOOK GREAT IN A PAIR OF *FLITTERIFIC MAPLE-BARK SLACKS!*
YEAH! THEY'RE REALLY COMFY!

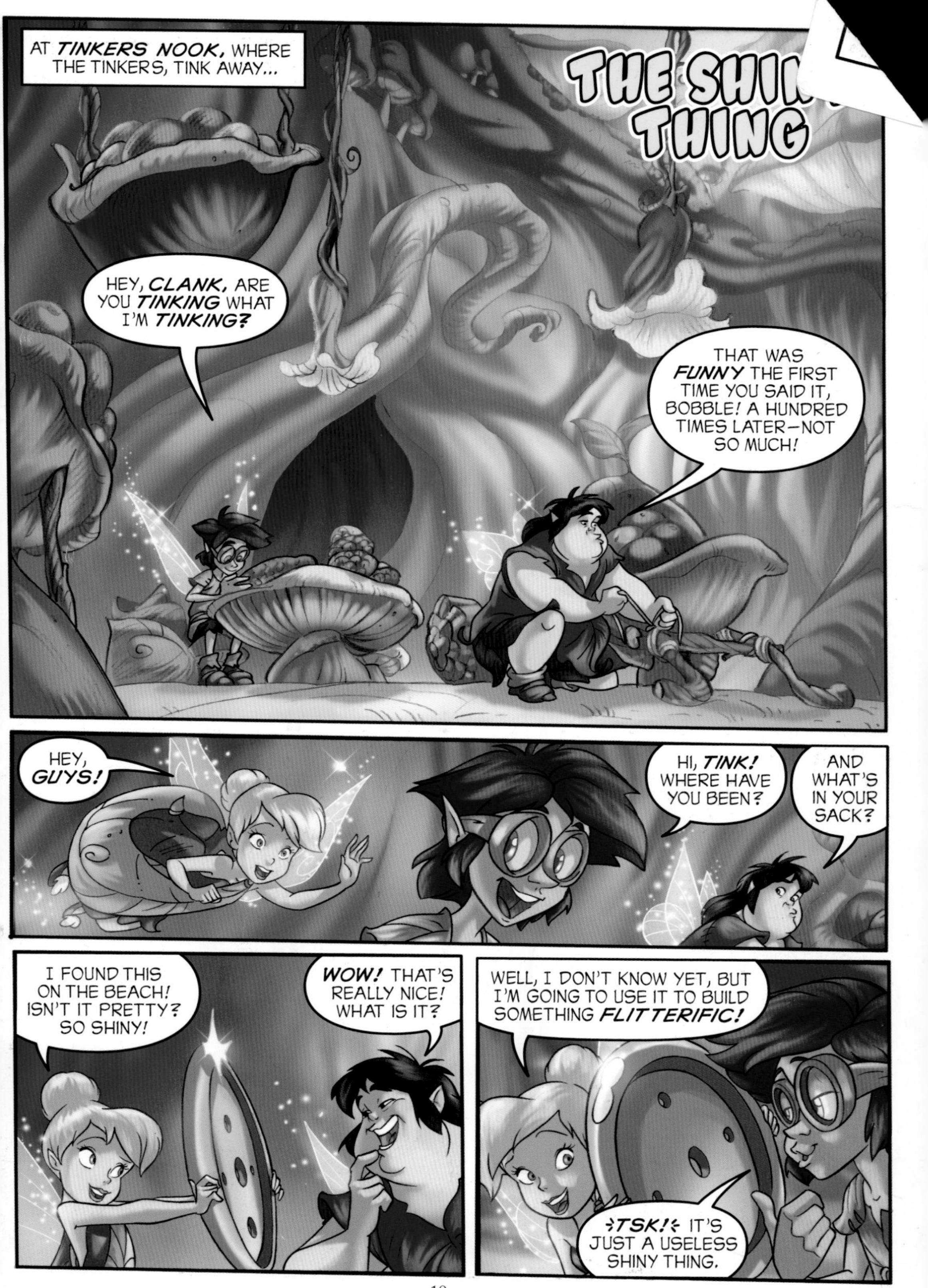
AT TINKERS NOOK, WHERE THE TINKERS, TINK AWAY...
THE SHIN THING
HEY, CLANK, ARE YOU TINKING WHAT I'M TINKING?
THAT WAS FUNNY THE FIRST TIME YOU SAID IT, BOBBLE! A HUNDRED TIMES LATER–NOT SO MUCH!
HEY, GUYS!
HI, TINK! WHERE HAVE YOU BEEN?
AND WHAT'S IN YOUR SACK?
I FOUND THIS ON THE BEACH! ISN'T IT PRETTY? SO SHINY!
WOW! THAT'S REALLY NICE! WHAT IS IT?
WELL, I DON'T KNOW YET, BUT I'M GOING TO USE IT TO BUILD SOMETHING FLITTERIFIC!
TSK! IT'S JUST A USELESS SHINY THING.

- 20 -

THE BUTTON BOUNCES OF A ROCK AND...

BOINK

WHOA...!

...SCOOPS TINK UP AS IT PASSES BY!

YOU JUST WON'T LEAVE ME ALONE, WILL YOU? WELL, MAYBE I KNOW HOW TO USE YOU AFTER ALL!

LATER...

SHE'S BACK!

HEY, GUYS!

THIS SHOULD BE INTERESTING...

AT LAST, TINK'S COME UP WITH THE PERFECT WAY TO USE THE BUTTON!

WOW! YOU DID IT!

THAT'S GREAT, TINK!

OH, YOU'VE GOT TO TRY THIS! IT'S SO MUCH FUN!

TINKER BELL KNOWS THAT NOTHING IS USELESS!

THE END

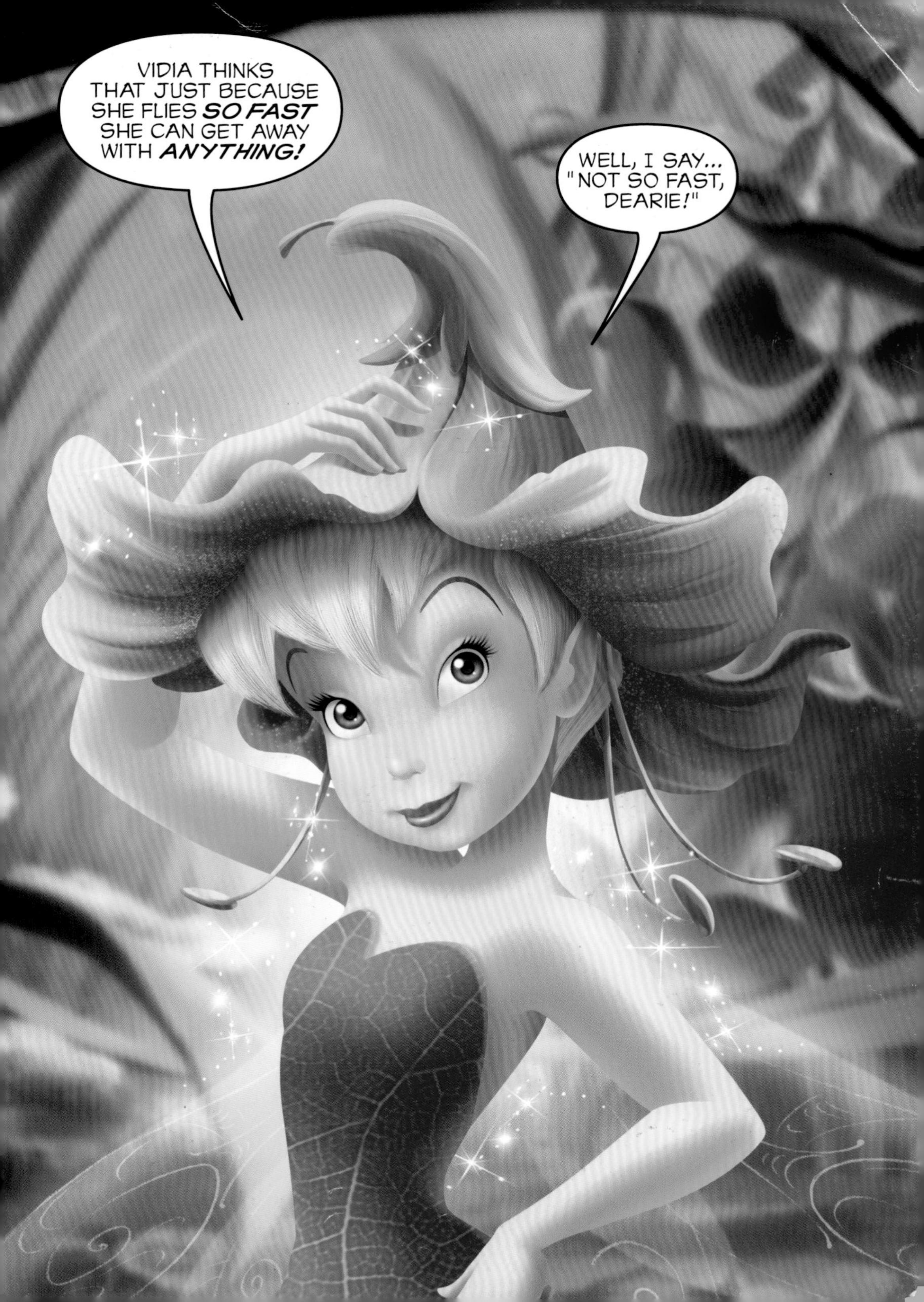
VIDIA THINKS THAT JUST BECAUSE SHE FLIES SO FAST SHE CAN GET AWAY WITH ANYTHING!
WELL, I SAY... "NOT SO FAST, DEARIE!"

A FAST-FLYING FAIRY SHOWS HER TRUE COLORS

...CARRYING BASKETS OF PAINT TO COLOR ALL THE LITTLE *LADY BUGS*...

WE BETTER HURRY, CHEESE! WE'RE RUNNING *LATE!*

...AND YOU KNOW HOW IMPATIENT THEY GET WHEN THEY ARE WAITING FOR THEIR *MAKEOVERS!*

⸨EEK!⸩

SWOOSH

!

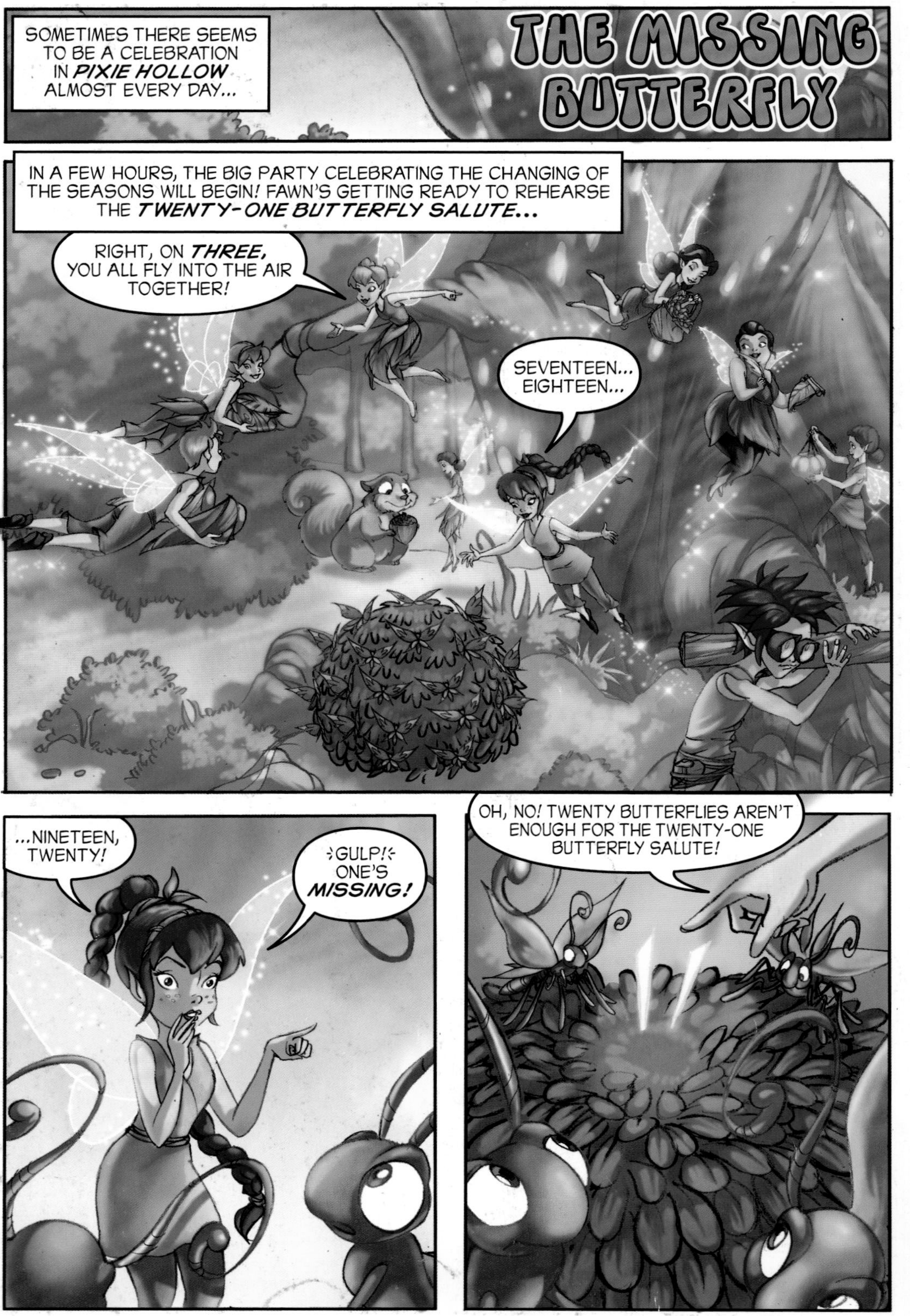
SOMETIMES THERE SEEMS TO BE A CELEBRATION IN PIXIE HOLLOW ALMOST EVERY DAY...
THE MISSING BUTTERFLY
IN A FEW HOURS, THE BIG PARTY CELEBRATING THE CHANGING OF THE SEASONS WILL BEGIN! FAWN'S GETTING READY TO REHEARSE THE TWENTY-ONE BUTTERFLY SALUTE...
RIGHT, ON THREE, YOU ALL FLY INTO THE AIR TOGETHER!
SEVENTEEN... EIGHTEEN...
...NINETEEN, TWENTY!
GULP! ONE'S MISSING!
OH, NO! TWENTY BUTTERFLIES AREN'T ENOUGH FOR THE TWENTY-ONE BUTTERFLY SALUTE!

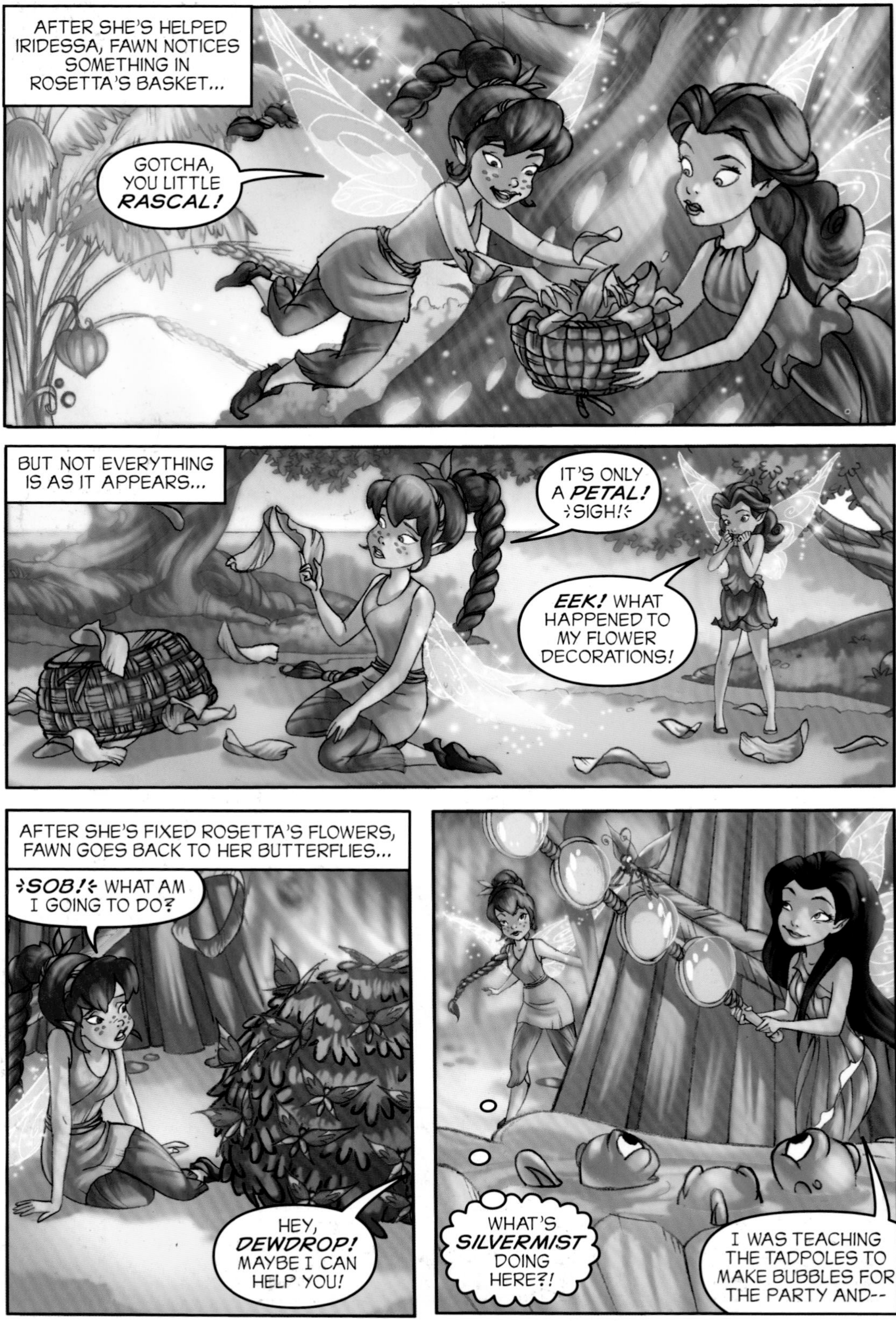
AFTER SHE'S HELPED IRIDESSA, FAWN NOTICES SOMETHING IN ROSETTA'S BASKET...
GOTCHA, YOU LITTLE RASCAL!
BUT NOT EVERYTHING IS AS IT APPEARS...
IT'S ONLY A PETAL! SIGH!
EEK! WHAT HAPPENED TO MY FLOWER DECORATIONS!
AFTER SHE'S FIXED ROSETTA'S FLOWERS, FAWN GOES BACK TO HER BUTTERFLIES...
SOB! WHAT AM I GOING TO DO?
HEY, DEWDROP! MAYBE I CAN HELP YOU!
WHAT'S SILVERMIST DOING HERE?!
I WAS TEACHING THE TADPOLES TO MAKE BUBBLES FOR THE PARTY AND--

THE BAD-MANNERED BLOSSOM

ROSETTA IS TAKING CARE OF THE SUNFLOWERS AND TINKER BELL IS KEEPING HER COMPANY...

HERE! THIS IS THE PERFECT SHADE, SEE?

UH-HUH... IT LOOKS THE SAME AS IT DID BEFORE TO ME.

I DON'T WANT TO HURT RO'S FEELINGS BUT I'M *BORED* OUT OF MY MIND!

PLIC

I WISH SOMETHING INTERESTING WOULD HAPPEN! *ANYTHING!*

OH, NO!

WHAT'S WRONG?

THIS POOR PETAL'S *SO PALE!*

I WAS HOPING IT WAS SOMETHING *EXCITING!*

LIKE A GIANT BEE WE'D HAVE TO RUN FROM...

DON'T WORRY, *SUGARCANE!*

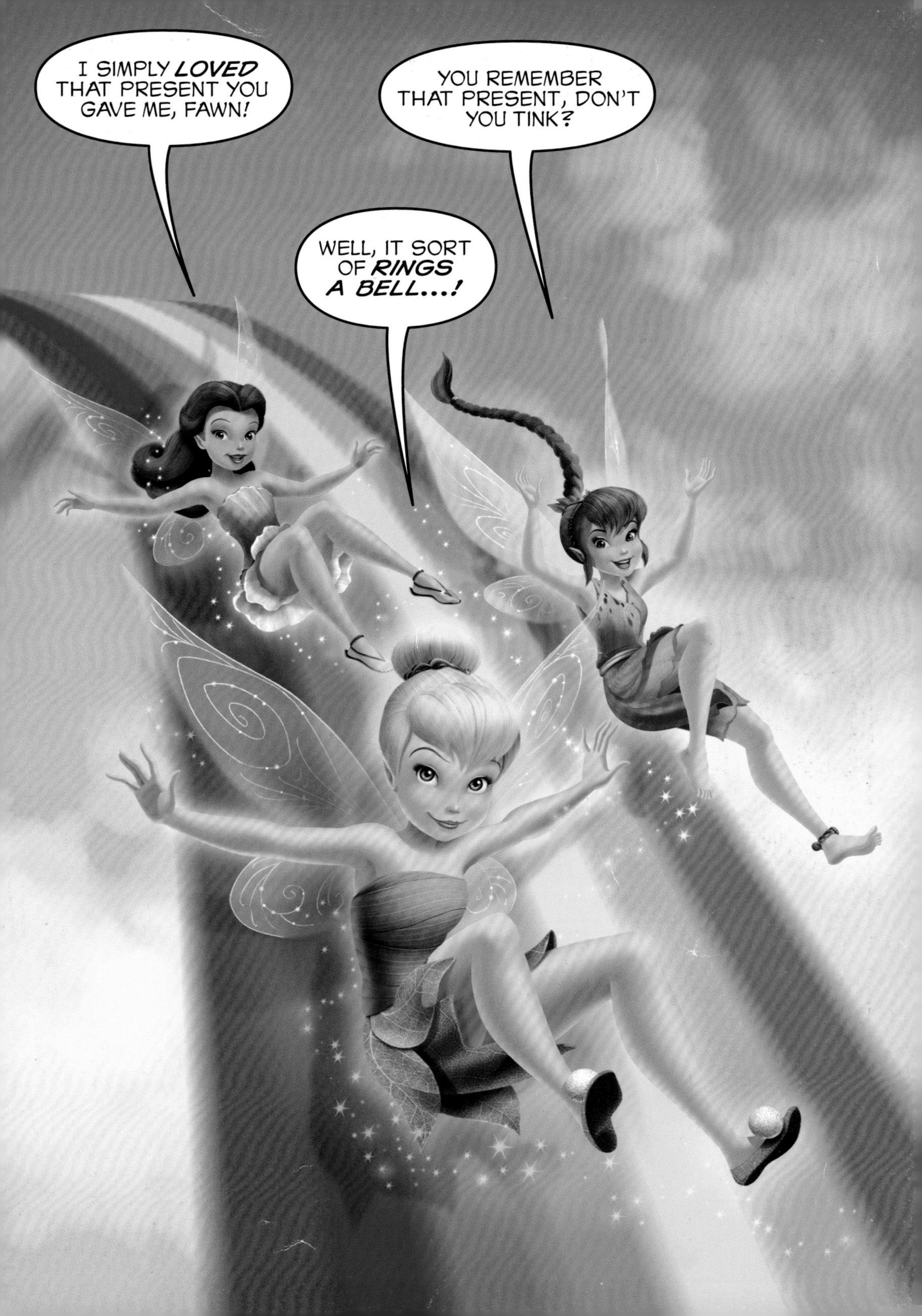

I SIMPLY *LOVED* THAT PRESENT YOU GAVE ME, FAWN!
YOU REMEMBER THAT PRESENT, DON'T YOU TINK?
WELL, IT SORT OF *RINGS A BELL...!*

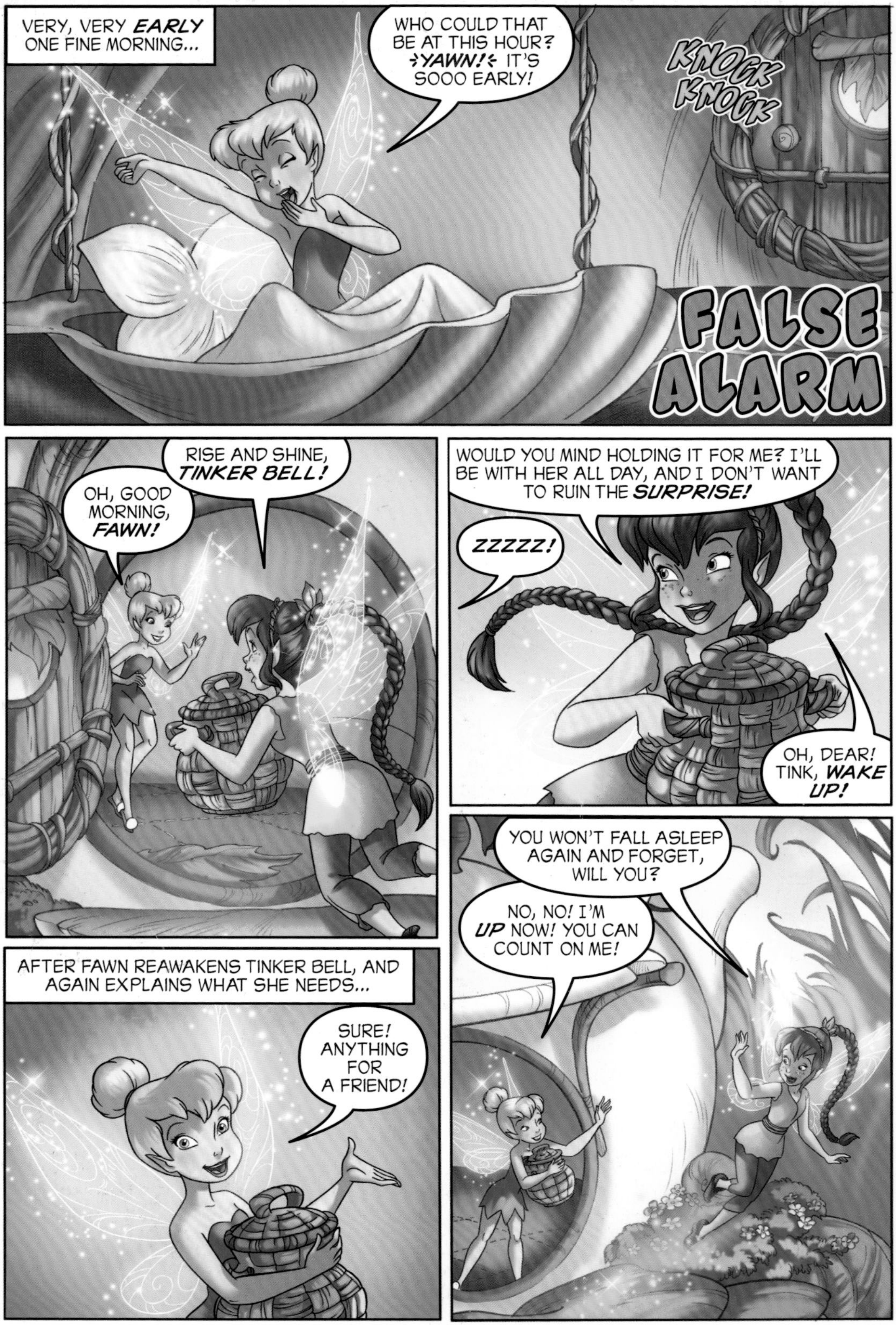
VERY, VERY EARLY ONE FINE MORNING...
WHO COULD THAT BE AT THIS HOUR? YAWN! IT'S SOOO EARLY!
KNOCK KNOCK
FALSE ALARM
RISE AND SHINE, TINKER BELL!
OH, GOOD MORNING, FAWN!
WOULD YOU MIND HOLDING IT FOR ME? I'LL BE WITH HER ALL DAY, AND I DON'T WANT TO RUIN THE SURPRISE!
ZZZZZ!
OH, DEAR! TINK, WAKE UP!
AFTER FAWN REAWAKENS TINKER BELL, AND AGAIN EXPLAINS WHAT SHE NEEDS...
SURE! ANYTHING FOR A FRIEND!
YOU WON'T FALL ASLEEP AGAIN AND FORGET, WILL YOU?
NO, NO! I'M UP NOW! YOU CAN COUNT ON ME!

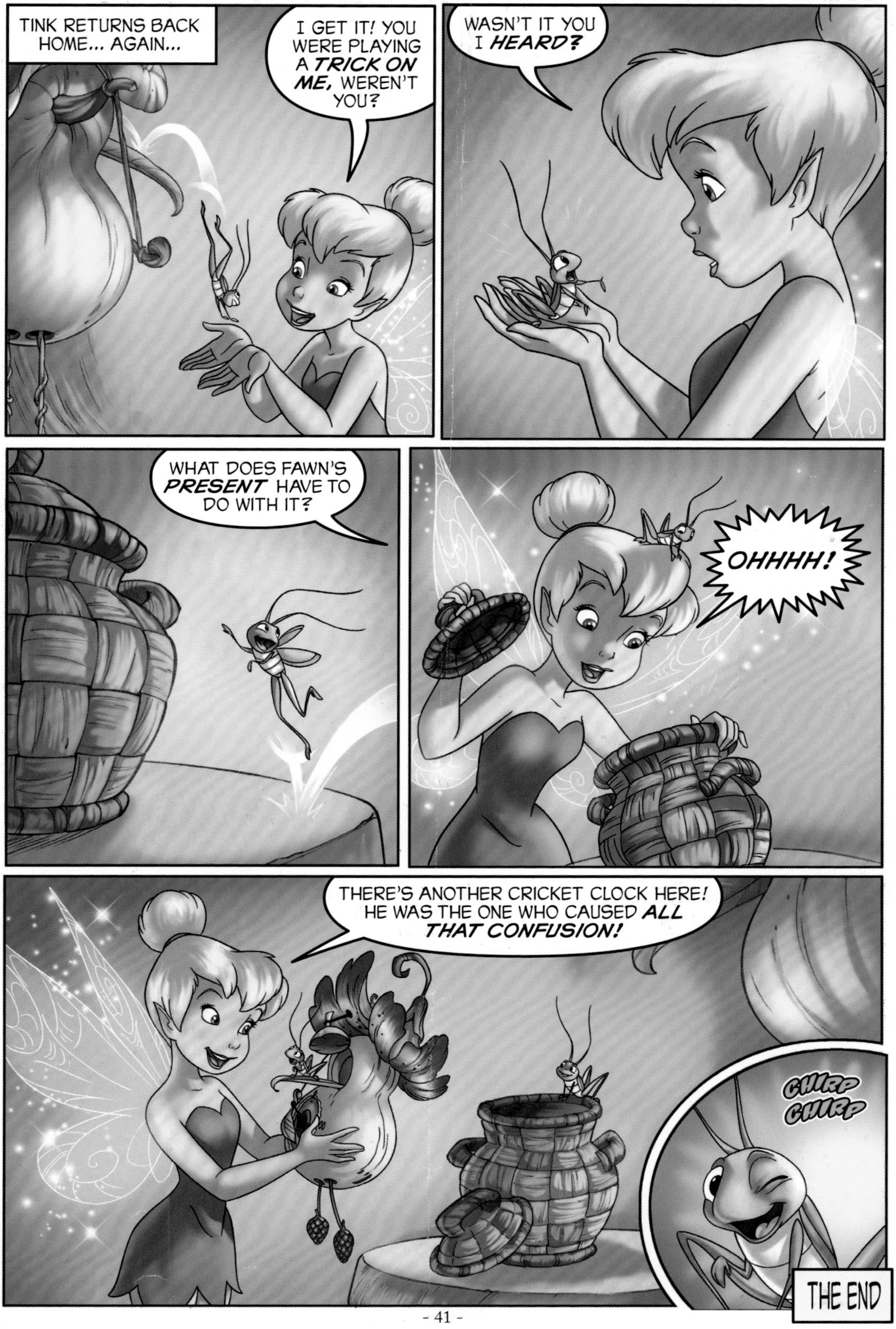
TINK RETURNS BACK HOME... AGAIN...
I GET IT! YOU WERE PLAYING A TRICK ON ME, WEREN'T YOU?
WASN'T IT YOU I HEARD?
WHAT DOES FAWN'S PRESENT HAVE TO DO WITH IT?
OHHHH!
THERE'S ANOTHER CRICKET CLOCK HERE! HE WAS THE ONE WHO CAUSED ALL THAT CONFUSION!
CHIRP CHIRP
THE END

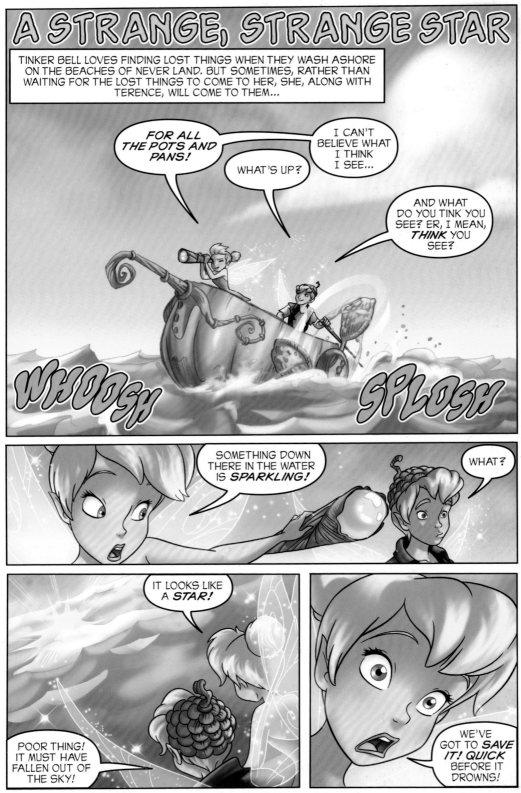

A STRANGE, STRANGE STAR

TINKER BELL LOVES FINDING LOST THINGS WHEN THEY WASH ASHORE ON THE BEACHES OF NEVER LAND. BUT SOMETIMES, RATHER THAN WAITING FOR THE LOST THINGS TO COME TO HER, SHE, ALONG WITH TERENCE, WILL COME TO THEM...

FOR ALL THE POTS AND PANS!

WHAT'S UP?

I CAN'T BELIEVE WHAT I THINK I SEE...

AND WHAT DO YOU TINK YOU SEE? ER, I MEAN, *THINK* YOU SEE?

WHOOSH

SPLOSH

SOMETHING DOWN THERE IN THE WATER IS *SPARKLING!*

WHAT?

IT LOOKS LIKE A *STAR!*

POOR THING! IT MUST HAVE FALLEN OUT OF THE SKY!

WE'VE GOT TO *SAVE IT! QUICK* BEFORE IT DROWNS!

- 45 -

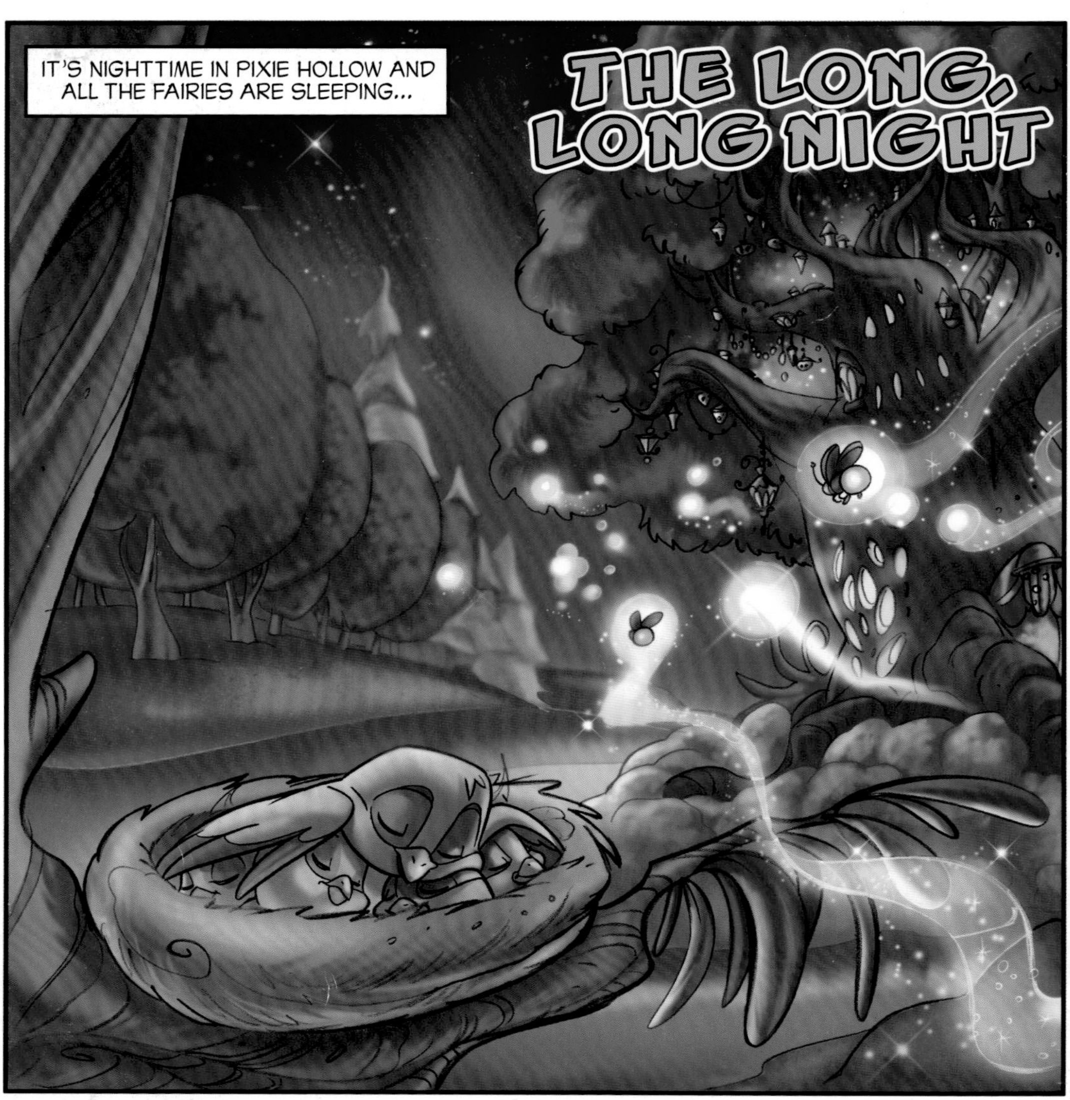
IT'S NIGHTTIME IN PIXIE HOLLOW AND ALL THE FAIRIES ARE SLEEPING...
THE LONG, LONG NIGHT

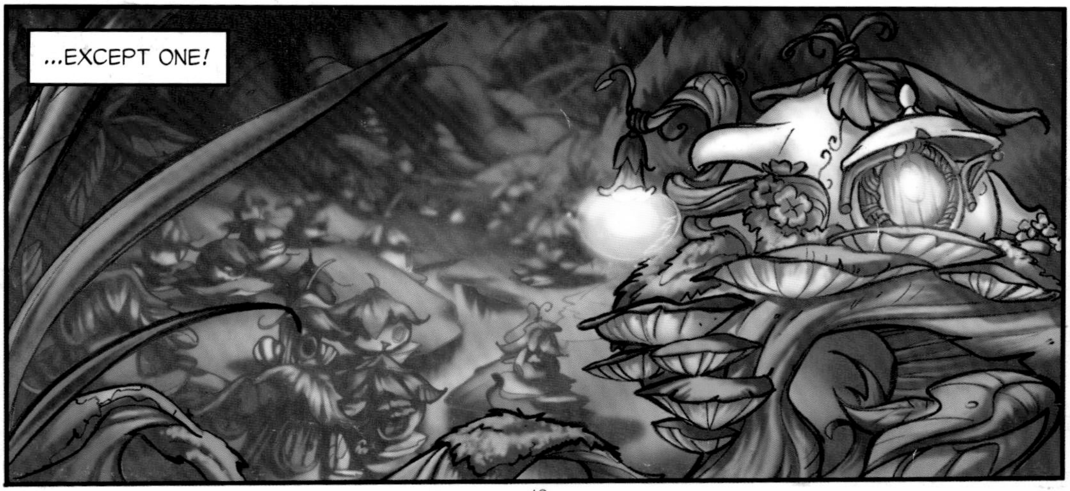
...EXCEPT ONE!

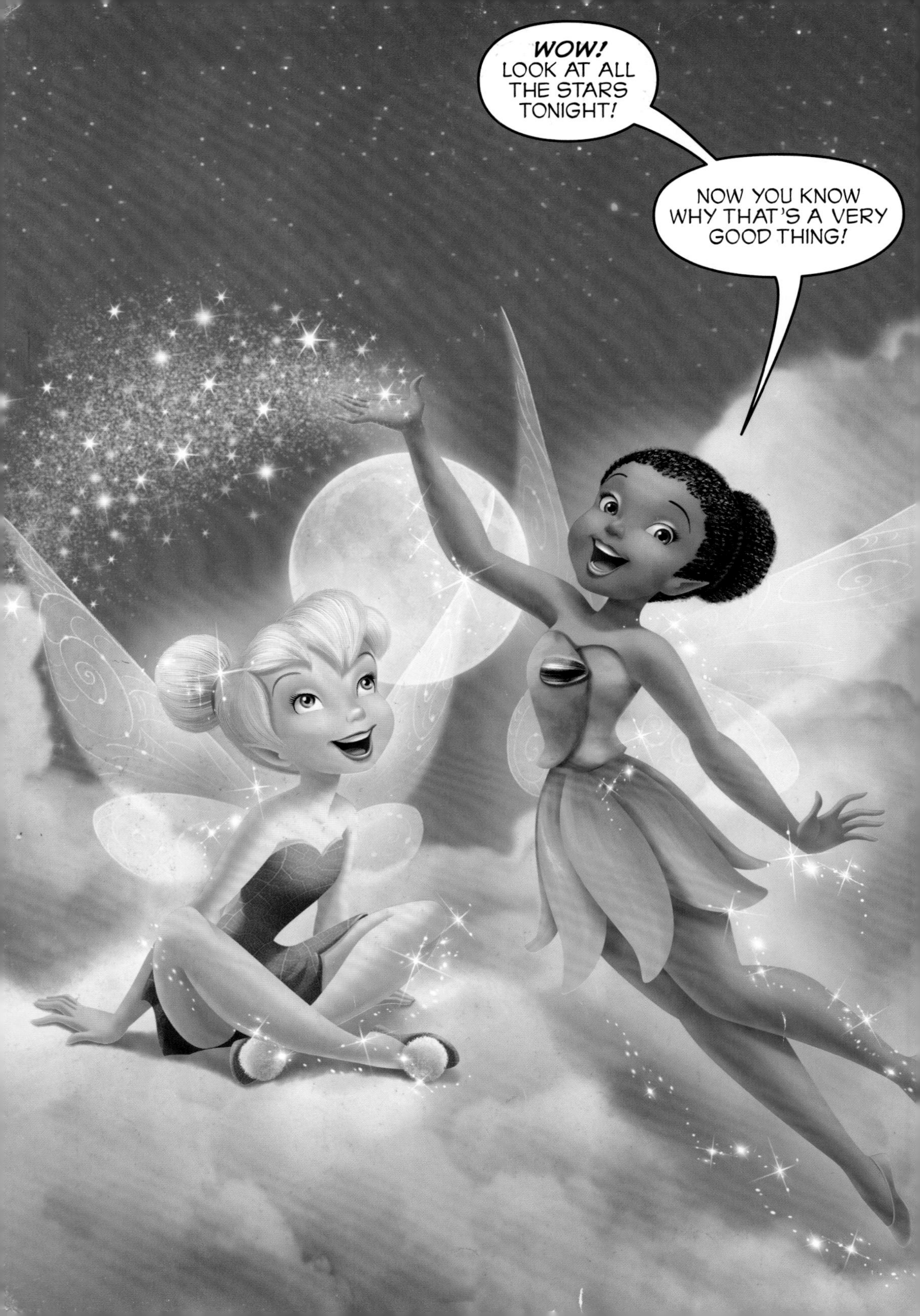
WOW! LOOK AT ALL THE STARS TONIGHT!
NOW YOU KNOW WHY THAT'S A VERY GOOD THING!

- 55 -

AN UNEXPECTED ADVENTURE

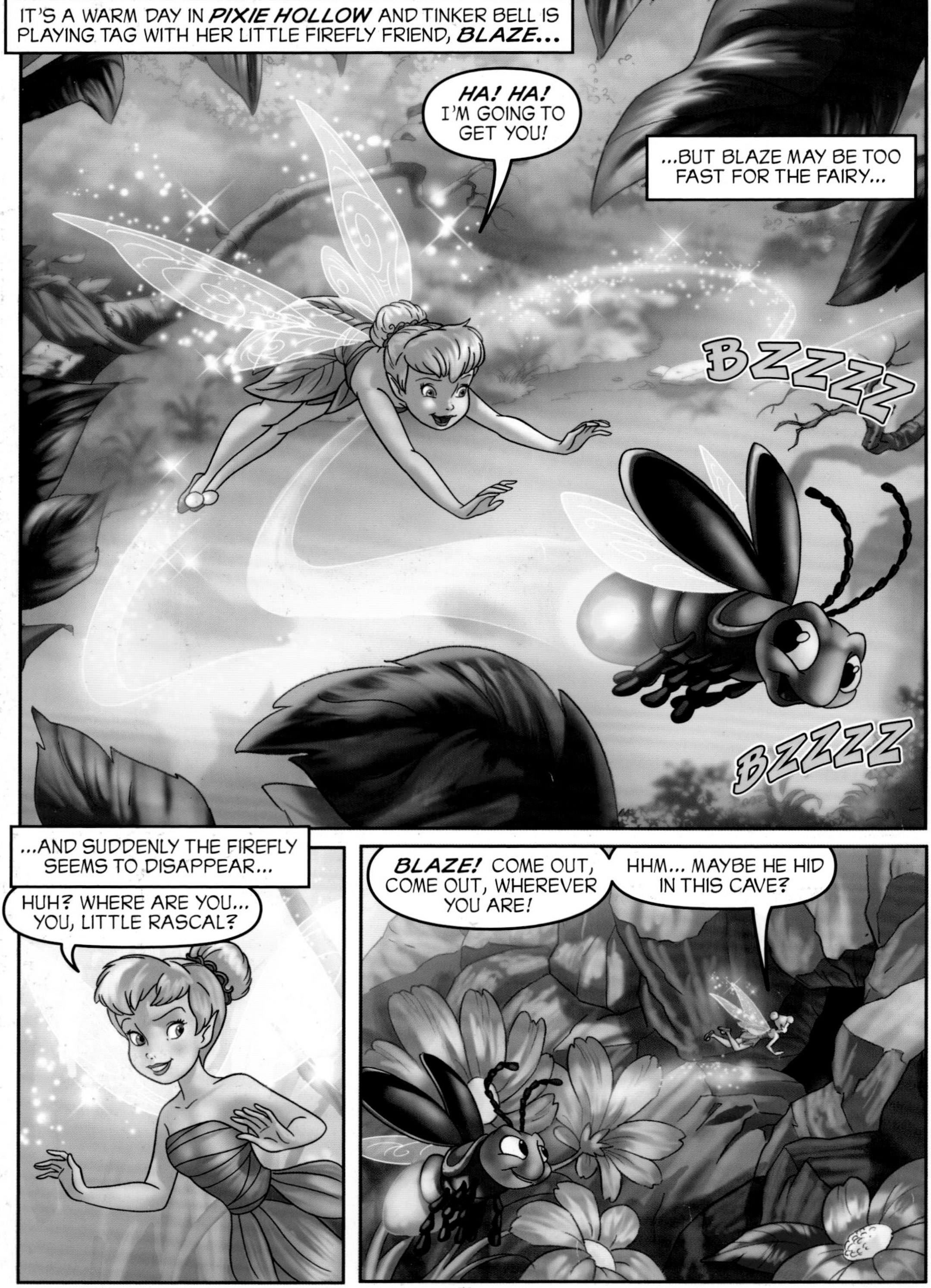

IT'S A WARM DAY IN *PIXIE HOLLOW* AND TINKER BELL IS PLAYING TAG WITH HER LITTLE FIREFLY FRIEND, *BLAZE...*
HA! HA! I'M GOING TO GET YOU!
...BUT BLAZE MAY BE TOO FAST FOR THE FAIRY...
BZZZZ
BZZZZ
...AND SUDDENLY THE FIREFLY SEEMS TO DISAPPEAR...
HUH? WHERE ARE YOU... YOU, LITTLE RASCAL?
BLAZE! COME OUT, COME OUT, WHEREVER YOU ARE!
HHM... MAYBE HE HID IN THIS CAVE?

- 60 -

DINOSAURS #1

"In the Beginning..."

Science facts combined with Dino-humor!

ERNEST & REBECCA #4

"The Land of Walking Stones"

A 6 ½ year old girl and her micro-bial buddy against the world!

THE GARFIELD SHOW #3

"Long Lost Lyman"

As seen on the Cartoon Network!

BENNY BREAKIRON #3

"The Twelve Trials of Benny Breakiron"

Benny Breakiron goes on the trip of a lifetime in his newest adventure!

THE SMURFS #17

"The Strange Awakening of Lazy Smurf"

Has Lazy Smurf been asleep for 200 years?

SYBIL THE BACKPACK FAIRY #4

"Princess Nina"

Nina and Sybil's Excellent Adventure Through Time!

Available at better booksellers everywhere!

Or order directly from us! DINOSAURS is available in hardcover only for $10.99; ERNEST & REBECCA is $11.99 in hardcover only; THE GARFIELD SHOW is available in paperback for $7.99, in hardcover for $11.99; BENNY BREAKIRON is available in hardcover only for $11.99; THE SMURFS are available in paperback for $5.99, in hardcover for $10.99; and SYBIL THE BACKPACK FAIRY is available in hardcover only for $10.99.

Please add $4.00 for postage and handling for the first book, add $1.00 for each additional book.

Please make check payable to NBM Publishing. Send to: PAPERCUTZ, 160 Broadway, Suite 700, East Wing, New York, NY 10038

(1-800-886-1223)

WATCH OUT FOR PAPERCUT𝗭™

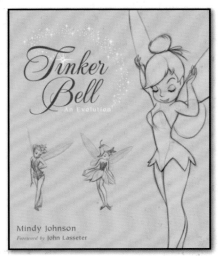

elcome to the fairy-filled fourteenth DISNEY FAIRIES graphic novel from Papercutz, those pint-size pixies dedicated to publishing great graphic novels for all ages! I'm Jim Salicrup, the full-time Editor-in-Chief, and part-time Fairy Aficionado around here!

Normally in this space I try to tell you a little bit about what else is happening in the wonderful world of Papercutz, but this time around, I have something else so exciting to tell you about, you'll just have to visit Papercutz.com to find out what's new and exciting at your favorite graphic novel publisher for all ages!

It's even possible you may already know what I'm going to tell you! After all, you probably love Tinker Bell just as much, possibly even more, than I do! Recently, an amazing new book came out all about the real-life history of our favorite Never Land fairy—"Tinker Bell: An Evolution" by Mindy Johnson and published by Disney Editions Deluxe. When I saw this beautiful book on the bookstore shelves, I knew I just had to have it! It's filled from cover-to-cover with fascinating facts and awesome artwork, all about how Tinker Bell was originally created and how she evolved to be the Pixie Hollow fairy we all know and love today.

What kind of facts? Well, for example… "How did Tinker Bell get her name? In J. M. Barrie's original version of the play 'Peter Pan,' the little sprite's name was Tippytoe, and she had speaking lines. But over time, Barrie decided that the fairy's expressions would be best voiced by musical chimes. During the early 1900s, vagabonds known as tinkers traveled from town to town, performing jack-of-all-trade repair services. Their arrival was hailed by the jingling of bells fashioned from tin that they mounted on their wagons. One of these 'tinker bells' was used to give Peter's fairy friend her voice in the original stage production, and the name stuck."

And there's so much more to be found in "Tinker Bell: An Evolution." If you're as curious about the history of Tinker Bell as I am, this is the book for you! Check either your favorite bookseller or library and ask to see a copy yourself. I know you'll love it!

In the meantime, keep believing in "faith, trust, and pixie dust"!

Thanks,

Jim

STAY IN TOUCH!

EMAIL: salicrup@papercutz.com
WEB: www.papercutz.com
TWITTER: @papercutzgn
FACEBOOK: PAPERCUTZGRAPHICNOVELS
REGULAR MAIL: Papercutz, 160 Broadway, Suite 700, East Wing, New York, NY 10038